CONTENTS

Chapter 1	3
Chapter 2	15
Chapter 3	20
Chapter 4	26
Chapter 5	30
Chapter 6	35
Chapter 7	39
Chapter 8	45
Chapter 9	55
Chapter 10	60
Chapter 11	66
Chapter 12	73
Chapter 13	76
Chapter 14	82
Chapter 15	86
Chapter 16	93
Chapter 17	105

Chapter 18	112
Chapter 19	119
Chapter 20	128
Chapter 21	138
Chapter 22	147
Chapter 23	158
Chapter 24	164
Chapter 25	180
Chapter 26	195
Chapter 27	203
Chapter 28	210
Chapter 29	222
Chapter 30	232
Chapter 31	239
Chapter 32	248
Chapter 33	253
Chapter 34	260
Earth's RPG Overlords	264
Chapter 1	265
Chapter 2	277

Level up - It's an RPG world.
Book 2 – Progression

CHAPTER 1

"Wow," said Leo softly. "These dudes really know how to make a tree house."

He, Jane, and Bradley stared at the treetop village from afar, marveling at the large, luxurious-looking houses nestled high in the boughs of the giant Redwood trees. A series of wood and rope walkways connected the various houses, and retractable rope ladders allowed access from the forest floor.

"It's beautiful," breathed Jane, her eyes sparkling with wonder. "Like a fantasy world."

"Umm… yeah," chuckled Leo. "That's because it is a fantasy world."

"True," conceded Jane.

"What are they?" asked Bradley.

Leo shrugged. "Hard to tell from this distance, but if I had to guess I'd say they were elves. Long blonde hair, tall, thin, pretty much full-on Lord of the Rings copies."

"You think they might be friendly?" questioned Bradley.

"Who knows?" answered Leo. "I suppose we

could approach them and see what happens."

"Why not?" agreed Jane. "Hell, with your martial prowess, I don't think we have anything to worry about."

"Not necessarily true," disagreed Leo. "For all we know, elves are all like a million years old and over Level 100 Warriors or Archers."

"I thought you must be around Level 100," said Bradley.

Leo chuckled. "Not even close, dude. Come on, let's go take a closer look. Don't try to be sneaky, let them see us coming, that way they should know that we aren't trying to attack them or nothing."

The three approached the distant treetop village, walking boldly and with purpose. Well, Leo did, Jane and Bradley tended to skulk a little, hiding behind him and trying their best to look totally non-threatening.

Which was pretty easy, because that's exactly what they were.

When they were still a few hundred yards from the village, Leo heard a slight rustle in the trees, and four people dropped from above to land lightly on the forest floor in front of them.

All four had their bows out and arrows nocked.

It was immediately apparent that Leo's guess had been correct. These were most definitely elves.

"Halt," commanded one of them.

Leo once again noted the phenomenon whereby the mouth of the person who was speaking did not correspond perfectly with the words he was hearing. He assumed it must be the System translating all languages automatically.

Which was nice. Because Leo sure as fuck did not speak elvish.

"We come in peace," said Leo. "We saw your beautiful village and simply wanted to greet you."

"Humans are not welcome in Eldrathil. Turn back. Now."

Leo did a quick scan of the lead elf and was surprised to see that he was only Level 22. A lot higher than any humans he had thus far come across to be sure, but if this was one of their warriors, Leo reckoned he didn't have that much to worry about. So, he decided to push his luck a little.

"Seriously, dude? Why the attitude? We ain't done nothing wrong, and we sure as hell ain't turning back, because we are heading that way," Leo pointed past the village. "Now, how about you lighten up a little, take us to meet your leader, and we'll see what happens. Trust me, we have all had a really shitty time of late, and the last thing we need is some hoity-toity elf telling us to fuck off."

"Wow, rave much?" whispered Jane.

"Hey, just trying to get my point across," responded Leo.

Before Leo could continue his diatribe, one of the elves stepped forward and spoke quietly into the leader's ear.

The lead elf stared at Leo, then he bowed deeply. "I apologize, my lord," he said, his voice filled with respect. "Please forgive me, I did not see you were tree-bound. May I ask the name of the Drus that has bound you?"

Leo raised an eyebrow. This was a surprise, and if the elf had not mentioned a Drus, Leo would have had no idea what was going on. But it obviously had something to do with his ring that contained part of Mossweaver's soul.

"Mossweaver," answered Leo.

There was a frisson of excitement amongst the four elves, and a couple of them repeated the male Dryad's name with reverence.

"My name is, Thalion," said the lead elf. "Please follow us, my lord. And you are welcome to bring your servants."

"Servants," spluttered Jane. "Just what the hell is going on here?"

"Long story," answered Leo. "Let's just say, not only have I got some mad skills, but I'm also tree-bound. Whatever that is. We'll talk about it all later."

They entered the area of the village and Thalion gave a high-pitched whistle. A wood and rope stairway rolled down from one of the larger tree houses, and Thalion gestured for them to follow him. The three other elves stayed on the ground, while Leo and his two companions clambered up the stairway behind the lead elf.

They stepped off the stairway and onto a large open balcony. Thalion kept walking, leading them to a connecting walkway that was strung between two trees. This one led to what was obviously the premier house in the treetop village. Not quite a palace, but very close to it.

Two guards stood outside the door, and Thalion bowed slightly to them. "I have brought a visitor to see the princess," he said.

The one guard shook his head. "No humans. You know the rules."

"He is tree-bound," interjected Thalion.

Both guards looked more closely at Leo, and then as one, they bowed deeply. "My lord," they greeted him.

The one continued to talk. "Please stay here, I shall inform the princess and then come back to fetch you."

Less than a minute later, the guard reappeared and bowed again. "Please, follow me, my lord," he requested. "Would you like your servants to wait here, or will they accompany you?"

"They can come with me," replied Leo, smirking slightly at both Jane and Bradley's snorts of disapproval.

Thalion opened a set of double doors and they walked through into a double-volume room with a vaulted ceiling, When Leo looked closer at the ceiling, he could see that it comprised of living wood. The tree itself had grown into an incredible arched structure. It was only then that he noticed the same could be said of the entire house. The floor and every wall were a living part of the tree.

At the end of the hall sat a woman on what could only be called a throne, although, like the rest of the building, it was part of the living tree itself. She stood as Leo and his companions approached, and walked towards them with such poise and grace it was almost as if she were gliding across the floor.

"Greetings, my lord," she said, her voice like silk. "It is an honor to welcome one of the tree-bound to our humble village. I am Princess Seraphina Evergreen."

Leo, not entirely sure how to greet actual royalty, decided a slight bow would do the trick. "Thank you, your princessness," he replied.

"Royal Highness," whispered Jane.

"Sorry, Your Highness," Leo corrected himself.

The princess laughed. "Please, the tree-bound need not stand on formality, call me Seraphina."

Leo grinned. "Cool, thanks."

"Please, could you and your servants take a seat at the table." Seraphina gestured towards a large round table at the side of the room. Around it twelve chairs. As she did so, a group of elves, both male and female, entered the room carrying trays of food and drinks. Thalion also joined them.

Seraphina," began Leo. "I must inform you that Jane and Bradley are not my servants, they are actually my newly met traveling companions."

They went to the table and waited for the princess to be seated before they took their seats.

"I must apologize," said the princess. "We assumed that someone who is tree-bound would naturally have servants. It is unheard of for them to travel alone. Usually, they would arrive with a much larger entourage. Maybe seven or eight at least."

"No, I don't roll like that," said Leo as he grabbed a plate and began to pile food onto it. Jane and Bradley followed suit. One of the serving elves placed a mug next to Leo and filled it with what appeared to be some sort of ale.

"No meat," noted Leo as he tucked into his plate of roasted vegetables, brown rice, and gravy.

"We do not eat the other inhabitants of the forest," said the princess. "That would be murder."

"Yeah, well I could murder a steak about now," mumbled Leo. "Or some fried chicken. Or chicken fried steak. Man, yum yum."

"My lord," interjected Seraphina. "It seems that fate has delivered you, a tree-bound, to our village in our time of need. I wonder if we could ask a favor of you?"

"Sure, ask away," mumbled Leo through a mouthful of food. "The worst I can do is say no."

"Our village has recently suffered a great tragedy."

"No shit," said Leo. "Like, so has my entire world."

Seraphina nodded. "Us too. We were Integrated without consent or knowledge. Almost all of our population has died, and the glorious Elvish Kingdom is but a shadow of its former self."

"I'm sorry," Leo apologized. "I sometimes forget that we humans weren't the only ones fucked over by the system. Please, what would you like me to do?"

Seraphina drew in a deep breath. "What do you know about dark elves?" she asked.

"Almost nothing," admitted Leo, refilling his mug of ale. "I think they're related to you guys in some way."

"They are, but more distantly than many think. Dark elves, also known as Drow, are a subrace of elves characterized by their affinity for the Underdark, and often a malevolent nature. They typically have dark or ebony skin, white or silver hair, and pale-colored eyes.

"They normally reside in a vast network of subterranean caverns and tunnels. They have adapted to the harsh conditions of this environment and developed unique skills suited for living underground."

"They are also skilled warriors and spellcasters," interjected Thalion. "And are often proficient with weapons like rapiers and crossbows. They may have innate magical abilities, such as the ability to manipulate darkness or summon creatures from the Underdark. We have a longstanding enmity between us."

"Okay, so now I'm an expert in dark elves," chuckled Leo. "What's that gotta do with things?"

"A few days ago, our village elder, who is the main healer, and the keeper of records, was kidnapped by dark elves. He was in the woods with two assistants searching for various magical herbs when they took him. They killed the one assistant, but the other managed to escape and tell us what happened."

"How do you know if he's still alive?" asked Leo.

"I would know if the spark of his life were extinguished," replied the princess. "The very forest itself would know. The chief healer and keeper of records is oft referred to as, the Caretaker. That is not only because he takes care of the elves in the village, but also because he provides the magic to ensure the trees continue to help us. Without him, our village will simply return to its natural state. The house will become trees once more. Not only that, healers are incredibly rare."

"Jane is a healer," said Leo.

"Truly?" asked Seraphina, her voice holding some obvious awe. "What Level, if you don't mind me asking?"

"I am Level 4," answered Jane.

The princess didn't comment, but the disappointment on her face was obvious.

"Problem?" asked Leo.

Seraphina frowned, pausing to think before she answered. "Elves are very long-lived," she said. "As such, our bodies, our metabolisms, and our life forces are very different from that of humans. As such, any healer below Level 30 could not be able to heal an elf. But it is not only that we lose such an integral member of our community, we also fear that the dark elves may use him for nefarious purposes. Sacrifice him in some dark ritual, or use his life force to power an evil summoning spell."

"Bummer," said Leo. "Do you have any idea where this Caretaker dude might be?"

"We know exactly where he is being held prisoner," answered Thalion.

"So why haven't you tried to rescue him?" asked Leo.

Thalion looked embarrassed. "To be honest, we are no match for the dark elf warriors. I am a mere Level 22 Archer and I am the highest level in the village."

"I thought you dudes were, like, awesome archers and fearsome warriors," said Leo.

"Why would you think that?" inquired the princess. "We are pacifists and vegans, why would we have a need for archery? The only reason we have any archers is that custom dictates every village has a small group of warriors in case it needs defending against possessed creatures, or evil beasts."

"Yeah, I suppose that makes sense," said Leo. "I must admit, I was hoping for more, Lord of the Rings, Legolas elves, as opposed to hippy commune circa 1960."

"Who is this Lord of the Ring?" asked Seraphina. "Is he also tree-bound?"

"Naw, he's ... it doesn't matter. Hey, Thalion, can you show me where your Caretaker is?"

Thalion nodded. "I will do so, and I

shall accompany you into the dark elves' evil establishment to help you and your servants ... sorry, companions."

"Hey, look I wanna be a come-with sorta guy," interjected Bradley. "But if a Level 22 archer reckons he's underpowered, then I very much doubt a Level 3 Fire mage is gonna do any good. But if you want me to, I'll come."

"As will I," added Jane.

Leo chuckled. "Thanks, but no thanks, guys. In fact, Thalion, after you've shown me where the healer dude is, I want you to split. I do my best work alone. Actually, up until now, I've done all my work alone. But I seriously don't need to be looking after anyone's safety. I'll go in, fast and quiet, and bring the Caretaker out. Well, that's assuming I can find him."

"I shall provide you with a magical amulet," said the princess. "It is known as a Verdant Moonlight crystal, this shall give you a special connection to the forest, granting you insights and protection in the enchanted realm. Part of this insight will be the ability to track the Caretaker and to sense when he is near."

"Sounds good," said Leo. "If you could do that, I'll be off as soon as. No time like the present and so on."

The princess stood up and went to an alcove behind her throne. She returned holding a small amulet attached to a sturdy leather thong. Without any further ado, she placed it over Leo's head.

Leo tucked it into his armor. "Thank you," he said. Then he frowned. "I don't feel any different."

The princess chuckled. "It will take a short time to adjust to your aura," she informed him. "Perhaps half an hour or so."

"Cool, Thalion, lead on."

Leo followed Thalion out of the throne room while the princess continued talking to Jane and Bradley.

CHAPTER 2

The forest stirred with ancient energy as Leo, flanked by Thalion, embarked on the clandestine journey toward the ominous lair of the dark elves. Princess Seraphina's enchanted amulet nestled against Leo's chest, emitting a faint, soothing warmth. As the amulet dangled, its magical resonance harmonized with the surrounding foliage, creating an ethereal connection between Leo and the forest.

Leo could feel the enchantment weaving around him, enhancing his perception of the natural world. Each step resonated with the pulse of the forest as if the ancient trees themselves were guiding him on this perilous quest.

Thalion, an elven warrior of considerable skill in his community, observed Leo with a mixture of curiosity and admiration. The human's connection with the enchanted amulet and the forest was a spectacle that even the seasoned elf found intriguing. Together, they moved as one, a silent duo weaving through the labyrinthine paths of the woodland, shadows blending seamlessly with the foliage.

Leo concentrated on his mana and his awareness expanded, detecting the nuances of the forest's life — the distant calls of unseen creatures, the rustle of leaves, and the delicate balance of mana weaving through the air.

The dense canopy above cast a patchwork of shadows on the forest floor as Leo and Thalion ventured closer to the realm of the dark elves. The air grew tense, and Leo's every instinct heightened. His senses, honed by so many battles in the tutorial dungeon, were on high alert.

A distant murmur reached Leo's ears, the subtle rustling of armor and hushed voices indicating the presence of a dark elven patrol. His eyes, sharpened by a combination of natural skill and the enhanced forest awareness bestowed upon him by the amulet, identified the faint glimmers of malevolent energy woven into the forest's tapestry.

"Patrol," Leo whispered to Thalion, gesturing toward the looming shadows. The elven warrior nodded, his gaze mirroring Leo's intensity. They crouched low, the underbrush providing a natural veil as they assessed the situation.

Leo's mana awareness painted a vivid picture of the patrol's movements. He could sense the rhythmic pulse of their enchanted armor, the faint hum of dark mana lingering in the air. These dudes were a different breed from the forest elves he had just met. Whereas the forest dwellers radiated a feeling of peace and tranquility, these guys exuded a feeling of malevolence.

A challenge lay ahead, and Leo's strategic mind worked swiftly to navigate the duo around the potential threat.

As the dark elves drew nearer, Leo made subtle gestures, indicating the precise path to circumvent the patrol. Thalion, normally accustomed to leading in stealth, found himself in awe of Leo's proficiency. The human moved with a fluidity and precision that defied the usual limitations of stealth, an unspoken dance with the shadows.

Silent as the night, they glided through the undergrowth, threading between the trees with a grace that belied the urgency of their mission. Leo's mana awareness became a guiding force, an invisible hand steering them away from the patrol's watchful gaze. Thalion, though a seasoned warrior, couldn't help but marvel at the human's uncanny ability to read the forest's arcane language.

The dark elves' patrol continued on their oblivious path, unaware of the elusive interlopers skillfully bypassing their watchful eyes. Leo and Thalion, now distanced from the potential threat, shared a brief nod, acknowledging the success of their maneuver. The forest, ever watchful, seemed to exhale a silent sigh of relief as the duo pressed forward, their journey through the shadowed domain of the dark elves continuing with an undercurrent of anticipation and excitement.

The looming entrance to the dark elves' underdark cave system yawned before them, a foreboding gateway to the heart of shadow and secrecy. Leo, his eyes calculating, surveyed the pair of vigilant guards stationed at the cave's mouth. He began weaving a plan to infiltrate without alerting the whole dark elf nation to the fact that he had infiltrated their dwellings.

He leaned in close to the elf. "Hey, Talion, if I take those guards out, you reckon you could create a diversion, draw that patrol we saw to you, and then get away safely?"

Thalion nodded. "I am a forest elf. This is my domain. They are subterranean dwelling morons. I will easily be able to lead them on a merry and fruitless dance."

Leo grinned at the elf's florid language. "Cool," he whispered as he equipped his bow and quiver. "Look, I'm gonna take these guys out. Then I'm gonna fire another arrow in the direction of that patrol, but I'm gonna Imbue it with lightning so it causes a loud explosion. They should come running. Let them see you, then you make tracks. Got it?"

Thalion nodded. "Would you like me to shoot one of the guards? I am proficient with my bow."

"I'm sure you are," agreed Leo. "But I got this. You just get ready to run. Hopefully, they'll reckon you shot the guards and then split. So, they won't suspect me of entering their shitty caves."

Again, Thalion nodded his understanding.

"Good plan, my lord."

Leo nocked an arrow while holding the second one in his draw hand. Then he Imbued them both with Wind to ensure they sped fast and accurately. Letting out his breath, he aimed and fired. Once, twice. Both shots so close as to almost appear to be a single shot.

Then he nocked a third arrow and Imbued it fully with both Wind and Lightning. Aiming in the general direction of the patrol they had seen a little earlier, he released. The arrow flew through the trees and then struck one of the trunks, exploding in a bloom of fire, the massive sound of the explosion echoing through the forest.

The patrol's reaction was instantaneous and Leo could hear them shouting as they sprinted through the forest towards them.

"Cheers, my friend," Leo said to Thalion. "Make sure you don't get killed. I'm outa here."

Thalion nodded as he set off toward the incoming dark elf patrol.

Leo moved into the caves, sticking to the shadows and moving as stealthily as he could.

CHAPTER 3

As Leo stepped into the dark elves' underground domain, the world transformed into a surreal spectacle. Bioluminescent fungi and mushrooms cast an eerie glow, creating an otherworldly tableau that painted the cavern walls with phosphorescent hues. The air itself seemed to shimmer with an evil, eldritch glow, giving the expansive network of caves a feel of subtle malevolence.

Moss-covered stalactites hung like ancient sentinels from the ceiling, their surfaces adorned with the ethereal glow of the fungi. The ground beneath Leo's feet was a mosaic of uneven terrain, a reminder that this subterranean world had existed long before his arrival, even though it most likely hadn't even existed before the RPG apocalypse.

As Leo ventured deeper, the glow intensified, revealing intricate carvings etched into the cave walls. Dark elven symbols adorned the stone, telling stories of a civilization enshrouded in mystery. The intertwining passages resembled a complex dance of shadows and light, offering both concealment and revelation.

The scent of damp earth and the distant murmur of an underground river added to the sensory symphony. Leo's every step stirred whispers in the darkness, a reminder that he was an intruder in a realm governed by a race both ancient and enigmatic.

In the subterranean maze, Leo's movements became a choreography of stealth, a silent ballet with shadows as his partners. His seasoned instincts guided him with the finesse of a practiced infiltrator, each step a calculated measure to avoid detection. The labyrinthine passages became his stage, and Leo, the lone performer, danced through the heart of the dark elven territory.

The tension heightened with each passing moment; an invisible string pulled taut by the anticipation of discovery. Leo's senses, both mundane and magically enhanced, detected the subtlest shifts in the air - a flicker of movement, a distant murmur - prompting him to alter his course with the fluidity of a shadow itself.

As he moved, Leo concentrated on the amulet, mentally bidding it to lead him to the Caretaker. And to his surprise, it responded and he could feel a subtle but unmistakable pull in a certain direction.

The path to the Caretaker's location revealed itself as a perilous journey, guarded by vigilant dark-elven patrols. Leo, ever the strategist, navigated the intricate dance of evasion and confrontation with the finesse of a masterful ballet. The subterranean passages became the stage for a silent performance, and Leo, the solitary dancer, moved with lethal precision through the shadows.

When he could, Leo evaded, but when there was no way around someone, he took to using his Bowie knife. Moving silently through the shadows and getting up, close and personal.

He was momentarily distracted when the knowledge that he was actively murdering sentient beings, and guilt and horror threatened to rear its head. But Leo tamed the feelings down and continued. They had taken the peace-loving elves' Caretaker and were set to do evil to him. He had to continue on his path to their destruction, and to hell with his pre-apocalypse feelings of guilt and dismay.

Another dark elf loomed up ahead of him. Leo once more looked for a way around him, but there was none. Stealthily, he crept forward, sticking to the shadows, and keeping low. Then, when he was close, he sprinted forward, Bowie knife at the ready. He slammed into the elf and put his hand over his mouth to prevent him shouting out.

Then the blade rose, and plunged downwards, cutting deep into the creature's subclavian artery. Leo held hard as the elf bled out, twitching and fighting. But in under a minute, he went still, and Leo lowered him to the floor, dragging him into the deep shadows as he did so.

He used the dead elf's tunic to wipe the blood off his knife and his hands and was about to continue when a thought struck him.

"Shit," Leo murmured to himself. "I haven't been looting these fuckers. Too long in the dungeon where I didn't have to."

He stepped forward and nudged the corpse with his boot. "Loot."

A System message flashed up on his screen.

You have received 110 gold coins, a dark elf rapier (Standard quality), and a dagger (low quality).

Leo also noticed that he had gone up a few Levels from the dozen Drow he had dispatched. "Cool," he breathed. "Level 54. Sure get a lot of XP for offing Drow. Hmm … I see I increased some skills as well. I'll check that out later. Right now, places to go, dark elves to kill, Caretakers to save."

He dropped his points into **Constitution** as he continued on his way.

As Leo inched closer to the imprisoned Caretaker, the tension intensified, the atmosphere thickening with the unspoken threat that surrounded him. Every passage held the potential for a confrontation, and Leo's senses remained on high alert, attuned to the subtle shifts in the ambient energy that heralded the presence of unseen adversaries.

The journey through the heart of the dark

elves' territory became a test of Leo's skill and instincts, a continuous struggle to navigate the labyrinth of dangers. With every passing moment, the anticipation heightened, weaving an intricate tapestry of suspense that enveloped Leo in the relentless pursuit of his quest. The imprisoned Caretaker, a beacon of hope in the darkness, beckoned, and Leo pressed on, his path fraught with the looming shadows of the dark elves' watchful patrols.

Leo could feel he was getting real close to the captive Caretaker, and a surge of anticipation enveloped him. Beneath the layers of his armor, the amulet nestled discreetly, its presence known only to Leo. A subtle current of energy, like a quiet hum beneath his skin, hinted at the proximity to the captive soul. Shadows wove intricate patterns on the cave walls, mirroring the intricate dance of emotions within Leo as he prepared for the inevitable confrontation lurking in the depths of the elven stronghold. He knew there was no way the Caretaker wouldn't be guarded, and it was more likely than not that he would not be able to simply sneak up and rescue him.

There was bound to be a bloody battle.

"Bring it on," whispered Leo to himself. "There's gonna be some serious ass-kicking happening soon."

In the quietude of the underground caverns, Leo's senses heightened, attuned to the subtle shifts in the environment. Every echo, every faint vibration beneath his armor, became a harbinger of the confrontation that awaited him.

In the heart of the elven stronghold, Leo navigated the labyrinthine tunnels until he entered a vast cavern. Numerous dark elven guards patrolled the area, their eyes widening in surprise at the unexpected intruder. In the center of the cavern, a sturdy cage held an elf that Leo could only assume was the captive Caretaker.

Leo, poised for battle, surveyed the surroundings with a steely resolve. "Well, well, what have we got here?" he quipped, a smirk playing on his lips. "A party in my honor? You dark elves really know how to throw a welcoming committee."

The guards, momentarily taken aback, fumbled for their weapons as Leo advanced confidently. "Don't bother with the invitations, I'm crashing this little shindig," he continued, the glint of challenge in his eyes. "Now, who wants to dance?" he asked as he equipped his war axe.

CHAPTER 4

As the first dark elf lunged forward, rapier in hand, Leo met the attack with a swift swing of his battle axe, the weapon imbued with a pulsating surge of mana. The blade cut through the air, severing the opponent's defenses and leaving him sprawled on the cavern floor. Leo wasted no time, swiftly conjuring a fireball in his free hand and hurling it at the next assailant.

The fiery projectile erupted upon impact, casting an eerie glow on the chaotic battleground. The acrid scent of burning flesh mingled with the metallic tang of blood as Leo engaged with the remaining foes. His axe danced through the melee; each strike a calculated display of lethal precision. The dark elves fought fiercely, but Leo's mana-enhanced prowess proved too **formidable**.

The cavern once shrouded in silence, now echoed with the symphony of chaos. The clash of weapons reverberated off the cavern walls, creating an intricate melody of combat. Roaring flames leaped and danced, casting ominous shadows that flickered and waned in rhythm with the ebb and flow of battle. The pained cries of dark elves pierced through the air, harmonizing with the metallic clinks of weapons meeting flesh.

Amidst the symphony of violence, Leo moved with the grace of a seasoned warrior. His axe carved arcs through the tumultuous orchestration, a conductor orchestrating a deadly ballet. Each swing was a note in a macabre composition, blending seamlessly with the crackling flames and the anguished cries of his foes.

Leo blasted the last elf with a mana bolt, then he stepped forward, using his axe to parry the elf's rapier thrust, and with a short swing, almost clove him in two.

Then he ran up to the cage that held the Caretaker.

But before he could confirm who he was, the forest elf shouted out a warning. "Behind you!"

Leo spun around to see a huge Drow coming at him from one of the interleading tunnels.

A quick scan showed he was at Level 59.

It would be Leo's most formidable adversary yet. The towering dark elf, his muscles rippling beneath obsidian skin, wielded a menacing war axe that glinted with malevolence. A daunting foe, larger, faster, and stronger than any Leo had faced before.

"Hey, big boy," yelled Leo as he shifted his axe, and Imbued it with even more mana, widening and lengthening the blades. "Welcome to the party."

The elf growled and kept coming, his eyes blazing with both anger and determination.

The air crackled with tension as the two axe-wielders circled each other, their eyes locked in a deadly dance. Shadows cast by the flickering flames played tricks on the cavern walls, creating an eerie backdrop for the impending clash. Leo's axe, imbued with swirling mana, gleamed in the dim light, contrasting with the dark elf's foreboding weapon.

The first strike came with a thunderous impact, the clash of metal echoing through the cavern. The dark elf's axe swung with deadly precision, but Leo deftly parried the blow, the force sending vibrations through his arms. Mana bolts crackled through the air as Leo retaliated, his own strikes guided by a combination of skill and arcane energy.

The dance of combat intensified as Leo and the dark elf traded blows, each maneuvering with a grace that belied the brutality of their conflict. Fireballs erupted from Leo's fingertips, casting bursts of searing light that briefly illuminated the swirling chaos. The cavern became a battleground of magic and steel, where each strike carried the weight of lethal intent.

As the battle reached its climax, Leo's resilience became apparent. The dark elf's strength was undeniable, but Leo's ridiculously high Constitution, a testament to his enduring fortitude, allowed him to weather the storm of attacks.

Wounds marked both of their bodies, but Leo pressed on, determination etched on his face.

The dark elf, realizing the tide turning, unleashed a final, desperate assault. Leo, his senses attuned to the ebb and flow of the battle, countered with a decisive strike. The war axe cleaved through the air, finding its mark, and the dark elf crumpled to the ground, blood pumping from a massive wound in the center of his chest.

Silence settled in the cavern, broken only by the ragged breaths of the victorious Leo. The sights of the battle – the flickering flames, the fallen dark elf, the sweat-soaked brow of the exhausted warrior – painted a tableau of the intense struggle that had transpired. The air hung heavy with the scent of burnt mana and the metallic tang of spilled blood.

In that quiet aftermath, Leo stood, battered and victorious, his resilience and skill prevailing against the formidable dark elf opponent.

CHAPTER 5

"Okay, my friend," said Leo, extending a hand toward the Caretaker as he walked over to the cage. "Let's get you outa there. My name's Leo, by the way. The princess sent me to get you back home."

Leo swung his imbued axe, its radiant glow slicing through the darkness as it shattered the lock. The cage door groaned open, and the Caretaker stepped into the dim light, his eyes reflecting a mixture of relief and gratitude.

"Thank you, Leo," the Caretaker whispered, his voice a faint echo in the cavern's depths. "Your bravery and martial prowess are the stuff legends are made of. I owe you my life."

Leo chuckled. "Hey, we're not home yet. Save the gratitude for later."

As the words hung in the air, Leo wasted no time. He swiftly moved to the fallen dark elves, their lifeless forms scattered across the cavern floor. His agile fingers deftly sifted through their possessions, accumulating a trove of spoils – gleaming gold, finely crafted crossbows, and an array of rapiers and daggers, each bearing its own dark history.

"Not sure what I'm gonna do with all this crap," mumbled Leo. "But it's free and available, so I'll keep collecting for now. Follow me, dude, and let's both try to be as stealthy as possible."

The eerie ambiance of the underground labyrinth persisted as they navigated the twisting tunnels. Shadows played tricks on the walls, whispering secrets of their encounter. Leo's mana awareness guided their path, a silent ally against the unseen dangers that lurked in the dark corners.

Leo tried to avoid the dark elves as they headed back towards the entrance. But by now it was obvious to the inhabitants that someone had entered their domain and was killing the inhabitants, so Leo found himself coming across more and more patrols.

The journey through the dark elves' domain unfolded as a perilous dance, Leo's lithe figure weaving through shadows with a deadly grace. The dimly lit caverns echoed with the clash of steel meeting flesh as he engaged in swift and calculated strikes, his imbued axe leaving a trail of fallen adversaries in his wake. The acrid scent of blood mingled with the metallic tang of combat, creating an atmosphere thick with tension.

Each encounter was a symphony of movement and violence, Leo's instincts honed by countless battles. The cavern walls bore witness to the balletic exchanges, where precision and speed were the keys to survival. The dark elves, caught off guard by the unexpected intruder, fell one by one, their futile attempts at resistance met with the ruthless combination of Leo's magic and his axe.

The spoils of war accumulated – the gleam of gold coins, the weight of finely crafted crossbows, and the variety of rapiers and daggers, each telling a silent tale of its former owner's malevolence. Amidst the chaos, the Caretaker observed Leo's prowess with a mixture of awe and gratitude.

As Leo pressed forward, navigating the labyrinthine tunnels with unwavering determination, the echoes of their journey reverberated through the caverns. The darkness, once an ally to the stealthy dark elves, now seemed to conspire against them as Leo and the Caretaker pressed on, bound by a shared quest for freedom.

"I was led to believe these dark dudes were better fighters than this," said Leo.

"Compared to the peace-loving forest elves, they are formidable warriors. Compared to you, however," continued the Caretaker. "They do seem to lack a little expertise."

"We're almost there," said Leo. "And if they got any sense, there should be a welcoming committee waiting for us at the cavern entrance."

Leo stored his axe, and equipped his bow and arrow, nocking and Imbuing one as they continued towards the exit.

As soon as they saw the light coming from

the cavern entrance, Leo took note of the posse of guards waiting for them - six well-armed Drow.

Leo drew and aimed for one of the elves standing in the middle of the group, hoping that his Lightning Infusion was now strong enough to take at least two or three of them out of the fight.

The arrow flew true and struck the target in the center of his chest. The ensuing explosion was both impressive and gross as bits of flesh, bone, and armor buzzed across the cavern like shrapnel, tearing into the elves standing next to the unfortunate minced target.

"Three down," said Leo in satisfaction.

He nocked again and fired, this one also struck its target, but although it blew him to bits, the explosion didn't take out any more of the Drow.

"Time to up close and personal," said Leo as he stored his bow and equipped his axe, leaping forward as he did so.

One of the remaining Drow fired his crossbow, but the bolt glanced off Leo's chest plate. The second dark elf also fired, and this bolt lodged in Leo's left bicep. Leo paused to rip the bolt out. Blood flowed freely from his wound, but his Constitution kicked in and within seconds the wound had closed up.

At the same time, Leo spun hard, wielding his axe like it was an extension of his own body. The blade decapitated the first elf, and hammered into the second elf's chest, killing both of them.

"Come on," said Leo to the Caretaker. "Let's

make like sheep and flock off outa here."
    The elf followed Leo out into the forest.

CHAPTER 6

Leo clambered down from the tree and frowned. "Those dark elf fuckers aren't that good at fighting, but they sure are tenacious. There's a couple of dozen on our tracks. Come on, let's move."

As Leo and the Caretaker pressed deeper into the forest's embrace, the rustling leaves beneath their feet played a silent symphony, echoing their elusive journey. Shadows danced among the ancient trees, shrouding the duo in a cloak of secrecy. The air itself seemed to hold its breath as the tension thickened with every step.

The forest, normally a place of tranquility, now bore witness to a clandestine chase. The vibrant hues of emerald and gold overhead offered little solace, as the duo remained acutely aware of the impending threat behind them. The dark elves, stealthy in their pursuit, followed like shadows obscured by the dense foliage.

The air was charged with an unspoken urgency, an invisible thread connecting Leo and the Caretaker as they navigated the terrain. The evergreen canopy above created a mosaic of light and shadows, painting a surreal backdrop to their escape. With each passing moment, the forest seemed to envelop them, offering its protection against the encroaching darkness.

Unbeknownst to the dark elves, Leo and the Caretaker melded with the essence of the forest itself. Leo's amulet, a gift from Princess Seraphina, hummed softly against his chest, attuning him to the ancient rhythms of the woodland. This connection granted them an advantage, allowing them to move with the grace of the natural world.

"Slow down," said Leo as they ran through a small gulley, bordered by thick scrub and trees. "This place is perfect for an ambush." He equipped his bow and quiver and directed the Caretaker to a place to hide. "I don't suppose I could convince you to take a couple of crossbows?" asked Leo. "I'll load them, you just point and pull."

The Caretaker shook his head. "I am sorry, Leo," he answered "But as a Caretaker and a forest elf, I cannot deliberately take another's life. Even one as corrupted and evil as the Drow."

"Fucking peacenik," mumbled Leo as he melted into the forest, ready to spring his trap. "Just get ready to run like hell when I tell you," he instructed the Caretaker.

In the heart of the forest, Leo and the Caretaker laid their ambush, hidden among the towering trees and the dappled sunlight. Leo's fingers caressed the string of his bow, anticipation coursing through his veins, as the Caretaker whispered to the wind, calling upon the forces of nature to aid them, to cast confusion amongst the dark elves.

The first dark elf stumbled into the ambush, oblivious to the imminent danger that lurked in the shadows. Leo drew his bow with practiced ease, the arrow imbued with Wind mana only to avoid alerting the rest of the Drow with an explosion. The arrow whistled through the air, finding its mark with unerring precision, sending the dark elf sprawling to the forest floor.

Leo managed to drop four more Drow before they even cottoned on to the fact that they were being ambushed.

"It's an ambush," yelled one of the Drow.

"No shit, Sherlock," mumbled Leo as he charged the next arrow with both Wind and Lightning. The arrow struck and exploded, taking out three more of the dark elves. Leo risked two more shots before he stored his bow and quiver. Those shots had brought an end to four more of the Drow.

"A dozen down," said Leo. "Not a bad day at the office so far. Hey, Caretaker, let's get the fuck outa here."

The two of them ran as fast as they could, dodging and weaving through the undergrowth.

"Shit, no time to collect my loot," complained Leo as the sprinted away. Leo was fast enough to leave the Drow far behind, but unfortunately, the Caretaker, although stealthy, was not the fastest, and the dark elves began to catch up, drawing closer by the second.

"Gonna have to stop and fight, dude," said Leo. They're gonna catch us for sure."

"Wait," said the Caretaker. "Let me try something."

He turned to face their hunters and whispered a few arcane words.

Vines slithered from the underbrush, ensnaring the dark elves and hindering their movements. Illusions danced in the sunlight, confusing and disorienting the pursuers. The forest itself seemed to come alive, aiding the duo in their struggle against the intruders, as the forest responded to its caretaker and benefactor.

Leo shook his head. "Seriously, dude. You got mad skills and instead, you just left everything to me."

"I did not want to aid in killing," responded the Caretaker. "However, now I am merely slowing them down so we can continue with our escape."

"You know, when we get back to the village, you and I need to have a serious talk," muttered Leo as they continued their escape, this time losing the dark elves completely.

CHAPTER 7

Tears glazed the Caretaker's eyes when he saw his beloved village come into view.

Eldrathil unfolded before him like a long-lost dream, a vision of home emerging from the shadows of captivity. The majestic Redwood trees, their towering forms adorned with vibrant leaves and cascading vines, whispered tales of ancient wisdom. The evening sun painted the sky in hues of amber, casting a gentle radiance over the treetop sanctuary.

Houses, seamlessly woven into the living tapestry of the trees, stood as harmonious dwellings. Each abode, adorned with blossoms and leaves, emanated an enchanting glow, a testament to the elven mastery in coexisting with nature. The walkways, crafted from supple vines and adorned with bioluminescent fungi, crisscrossed through the village like veins, connecting the ethereal houses in a dance with the forest breeze.

As the Caretaker stepped onto the pathways, he experienced an overwhelming sense of relief. The cool breeze carried the sweet fragrance of elven blooms, intertwining with the natural scents of the forest. He marveled once more at the intricacy of his native elven architecture, where every house was a living part of the trees, a harmonious blend of nature, magic, and craftsmanship.

The laughter of elven children echoed through the air, a melody of innocence that resonated with the timeless essence of Eldrathil. The sense of peace, so starkly contrasting with the darkness of his imprisonment, wrapped around the Caretaker like a comforting embrace.

"Home again, home again, jiggety-jig," said Leo.

"You have no sense of decorum," said the Caretaker. "This is an emotional moment for me." But his seeming scolding was offset by his smile and his obvious expression of gratitude.

Princess Seraphina, adorned in an elegant gown woven from living vines, awaited their return. Her eyes, a reflection of the wisdom etched into the ancient trees, sparkled with gratitude as Leo and the Caretaker entered the throne room, announced by the ever-present guards.

The princess, flanked by Thalion, Jane, Bradley, and other elves, stepped forward to greet them.

"Lord Leo, you have returned with our beloved Caretaker," Seraphina spoke with a regality softened by genuine warmth. "You have our deepest thanks. I hereby declare you to be, a Friend of the Elves, a title never before given to a human."

"Cool," said Leo with a grin. "Just doing what I can, Your Highness. Turns out, the Caretaker and I make a pretty good team. Well, in that, I do all the killing and rescuing, and he refuses to hurt anyone or take a life. But apart from that, we're pretty much exactly the same."

There was a ripple of subdued laughter, mainly from Jane and Bradley who got Leo's heavy-handed sarcasm. The elves merely laughed out of politeness, as they sensed Leo was joshing, but they weren't sure what about.

In an impromptu celebration, the elves orchestrated a feast, and a large open platform strung between four trees that served as the village square transformed into a lively revelry. Elven music echoed through the boughs, and the air buzzed with the laughter and joy of the woodland inhabitants. The banquet tables were adorned with fruits, nuts, and delicacies crafted from forest ingredients.

Leo still wasn't enamored with the vegan food, but the alcohol was superb and a host of servers ensured that his goblet never ran dry.

As the festivities unfolded, Princess Seraphina approached Leo, a goblet of elven nectar in hand. "To our Friend of the Elves," she toasted, her eyes reflecting genuine camaraderie. "I wonder, my Lord," she continued. "Could we convince you to stay here at Eldrathil with us, as our protector and friend?"

Leo raised an eyebrow. "Sorry, princess," he replied. "No can do. Look, if you guys are gonna survive this new fucked up world we find ourselves in, you gonna have to learn how to defend yourselves. Or at least be prepared to. You see, getting me to do your dirty work, and condoning it, is no different than doing it yourself. You can't be all – we don't kill – and then send me out to kill. In other words, you can't have your cake and eat it. I don't mean to sound like a dick, I really like you guys, but you have to wake up to the harsh reality here."

Seraphina frowned. "There is truth in what you say," she admitted. "And it was presumptuous of me to ask you to protect us. On the plus side, however, we are extremely isolated, and with the Caretaker's skills, the forest will help hide us. Hopefully, that should be enough to keep us from harm."

"Here's to hope," Leo replied, clinking his goblet against hers. The elven nectar, a blend of natural flavors, left a lingering sweetness on their lips.

Jane and Bradley, amidst the celebration, joined Leo. "Well, Leo, looks like you're a hit with the elves," Jane teased, her eyes sparkling with amusement.

"I'm a hit everywhere, Jane. Elves, humans, you name it," Leo retorted. "Except for fucking murder-bunnies. Although that seems to have changed."

Jane chuckled. "Not sure I get that reference," she admitted. "But whatever. So, what's the plan?"

Leo shrugged. "Get drunk, sleep it off, then

continue our journey. I'd like to find my parents, but I got no idea where they might be. This new Earth is totally different from what it used to be." Leo took another sip of his drink and then did a double take. "Hey, I just remembered, I got a map of this place in my Inventory. Slipped my mind."

Leo willed the map to appear in his hand – but nothing happened. "Shit, what's going on?" he quipped as he checked his Inventory. Sure enough, the map was listed there. Again, he willed it to appear. And this time it came up on his screen. But what he saw was a huge disappointment.

"What?" asked Jane, noting the obvious expression of distress on Leo's face.

"Fucking stupid map. It's all grayed out. The only places I can see are the places I've already been. Fat lot of good that is. I wanna know where to go, not where I've just gone."

"Never mind," said Jane. "We'll find a way. Ask at any towns and villages we come across, scout areas out. We'll find them."

"Yeah, I suppose. Eventually," conceded Leo.

The night progressed with tales of adventure and shared laughter. The elves, once reserved, embraced the trio as newfound friends. The scents of enchanted blossoms and the sounds of elven songs intertwined, creating a tapestry of harmony in the heart of the treetop village.

The next morning, after sleeping in a little late, Leo and his two companions were ready to set off.

Before they did so, Princess Seraphina

approached Leo. "Friend of the Elves," she said "We are forever grateful. You will always be welcome in Eldrathil."

Leo, a hint of melancholy in his eyes, replied, "I appreciate that, Your Highness. But our journey continues. There are more realms to explore, more adventures to be had. Places to go and people to kill, as they say in the classics."

With a final exchange of gratitude, Leo, Jane, and Bradley bid farewell to the elves. The village slowly disappeared behind the thick foliage as they ventured once more into the mysteries of the RPG world, leaving the celebration's echoes to linger in the tranquil embrace of Eldrathil.

CHAPTER 8

"Stop," commanded Leo, his voice pitched low but still full of urgency.

"What?" asked Jane.

"We got incoming," replied Leo. "Something big and bad is heading our way."

"How do you know?" asked Bradley.

"Mana sense," answered Leo as he equipped his bow and quiver, nocking and charging an arrow to full capacity with both Wind and Lightning.

They could hear the creature rampaging through the forest as it approached at speed, breaking branches and smashing down trees as it ran. As soon as it came into view, Leo used Identify.

Forest Drake – (Level 62)
Strengths:

Camouflage: The Forest Drake could seamlessly merge with its surroundings, making it challenging to detect.

Poisonous Breath: The creature could exhale a toxic mist, capable of causing paralysis if not evaded.

Razor-sharp Claws: Its limbs were equipped

with razor-sharp claws, capable of rending through armor.

Agile Movement: The Drake possessed swift and agile movements, making it a challenging target.

Weaknesses:

Fire Vulnerability: Despite its forest adaptation, the Forest Drake had a vulnerability to fire-based attacks.

Limited Range: The poisonous breath had a limited range, requiring the Drake to be in close proximity to deploy it effectively.

The Forest Drake, a creature of majestic enchantment, seamlessly blends into the ancient woodland with moss-covered bark-like scales of varying green and brown hues. Its eyes gleam with otherworldly intelligence, complemented by antler-like horns emitting a subtle luminescence. Swift and lethal, its obsidian-sharp claws and delicate, mosaic-like wings showcase both power and grace. The tail, armored and thorn-adorned, symbolizes dominance over the woodland. Vulnerable to fire-based attacks, the Forest Drake rules as a guardian and predator, its existence is intricately woven into the enchanted tapestry of the ancient forest.

"Okay, I've fought something similar to this before," announced Leo. "It's vulnerable to fire, but be careful, it has a poisonous breath attack. Sorta like mustard gas. But it's short ranged, so just stay away from it and you should be safe. Well, safe-ish. Bradley, hit it with fireballs whenever you can. Jane, stay way back, heal us if we need it. Now let's rock and roll."

He aimed and fired, the arrow striking the drake on the side of its head and exploding with enough force to tear one of its ears off. It roared in anger and pain and immediately let forth a cloud of poisonous gas. But all three were still out of range, so the gas simply dissipated into the surrounding forest.

Leo fired off another arrow, this one striking the drake in the chest. This one exploded well, but the beast's thick armored skin shrugged off the bulk of the blast.

"Bradley, any time you feel the need," yelled Leo. "Hit this motherfucker with a few fireballs."

A golf ball sized fireball arced through the air and splashed on the drake's neck. It had absolutely zero effect.

Leo arched an eyebrow. "Seriously, dude? Is that it?"

"Hey, I'm sorry we can't all be Level twenty thousand, super-fucking-human killing machines," yelled Bradley. "I already told you, man, I'm a Level fucking 3 fire mage."

"Yeah, sorry," apologized Leo as he wound up a white-hot fireball the size of a wrecking ball and launched it at the drake.

The flaming ball of plasma hit the drake on

its left wing and burned a massive hole straight through it.

"He shoots, he scores, shouted Leo as he readied another fireball. This one struck the drake in the middle of its forehead, blinding it and driving it backward, squealing in agony.

Leo equipped his axe, imbuing the blade at the same time as he sprinted forward. Leaping high in the air, he brought the blade down in a vicious arc, hitting the drake on the top of its head, right between the two horns. The Imbued blade struck deep, smashing through the beast's skull and slicing into its brain.

The drake shuddered briefly and then collapsed, releasing a cloud of poisonous gas as it did. The gas enveloped Leo, burning his eyes and any exposed skin. He held his breath to prevent any getting into his lungs, but it still hurt like hell.

Jane started running towards him, but he waved her back. "No," he said. "Still gas in the air, and trust me, it will fuck you up good and proper."

Leo moved out of the cloud and then bent over, hacking and coughing. Jane jogged over to him, preparing to use her healing. But as she watched, Leo's incredibly high Constitution was already knitting the burned skin back together, and clearing the toxins from his eyes.

"That's incredible," said Jane in amazement. "Just how high is your Con?"

"High enough," answered Leo. "That still fucking hurt though."

"Nice one, boss," interjected Bradley. "Sorry about the rather ineffectual assist, but on the plus side, because I was involved, I got a couple of Levels outa that. I'm now a Level 5 fire mage."

"Good," responded Leo. "I also got a Level, plus I got a couple when we were running from the dark elves as well. Killed quite a lot of them. Guys," he continued. "We need to talk. You are both, and I don't mean to be an asshole, but you are useless. Hold on, let me get my loot before we have a chat. Bradley you too. Jane, not sure how the System works, I assume you were part of the team so you get some loot as well. Did you get any levels?"

Jane shook her head. "No, I think you actively have to participate to Level up. I can try looting, let's see."

Leo touched the drake's body. "Loot." His Inventory showed he had five pieces of cured drake hide, two vials of poisonous gas, three pieces of drake meat, and two claws. "You know, I'm not sure what I'm gonna do with all this crap I'm getting. Hopefully, there's some kinda System shop, merchants, or someone that will pay us for it. Bradley, what you get?"

"Meat, hides, some teeth."

"Cool. Jane?"

Jane shook her head again. "Nothing."

"No worries," said Leo. "It's pretty much all crap anyway. Let's get away from the body before it attracts more uglies. Then, as soon as we find a good place to camp, we need to talk about me training you guys up, okay?"

"That would be awesome," said Bradley. "So, we'll be, like, disciples."

"Bradley," sighed Leo.

"Yes."

"Fuck off."

Leo led the way, chucking his 15 points into Strength because – why not? He checked out his Stats as they walked, and he noticed he had gained an official title.

Character Name: Leo Armstrong (Human)

Class: *Stormcaller Archmage-Hunter*

Titles: Friend of the Elves

Level: 57

Experience Points (XP): 6200000/6000000

Stats:
- **Strength (STR):** 549
- **Dexterity (DEX):** 504
- **Constitution (CON):** 834
- **Intelligence (INT):** 504
- **Wisdom (WIS):** 594
- **Charisma (CHA):** 453

Stat points available - 0

Note - 5 Stat points are made available during each Level gained.

Skills:

- **Axe Throwing (Level 12):** subject is skilled in throwing axes accurately, dealing damage from a distance.
- **Survival (Level 15):** subject can navigate through wilderness, track animals, and find resources efficiently.
- **Archery (Level 23):** subject is proficient with a bow, allowing him to shoot arrows with power and accuracy.
- **Camping (Level 5):** subject excels at setting up camps, building fires, and surviving in outdoor environments.
- **Cooking (Level 3):** The subject can prepare simple and nutritious meals using outdoor ingredients.
- **Axe Wielding (Level 26):** subject can wield an axe with a good degree of proficiency.
- **Lighting Infusion (Level 16):** subject can infuse his arrows with the power of a Thunderbolt.
- **Wind Infusion (Level 18):** subject can infuse his arrows with the power of the Wind, this allows the arrow to travel further, faster and with more accuracy.

Spear Wielding (Level 12): subject is now aware of which end of the spear is the dangerous one.

Mana Manipulation & Core Control (Level 33): subject can now actively affect external mana.

Dagger Wielding (Level 4): subject can now use his dagger to deal death.

Inventory:

- **Weapons:**
  - Throwing Axes (x2)
  - Battle Axe
  - Bowie Knife
  - Bow of Storms (Soulbound)
  - Quiver of Antiquity (Soulbound)
  - Starforged Spear (Soulbound)

- **Armor:**
  - Leather tunic with metal scales (Self-repairing, self-cleaning)
  - Vambrace (x2) (Self-repairing, self-cleaning)
  - Reinforced Leather Boots (Self-repairing, self-cleaning)
  - Stout leather trousers with metal scales (Self-repairing, self-cleaning)

- **Consumables:**
  - Healing Potion (5)
  - Rations (3 days)

- **Tools:**
  - Flint and Steel
  - Compass
  - Climbing Gear

- **Miscellaneous:**
  - Map of the RPG Earth
  - 420 gold coins
  - Verdant Moonlight Amulet (Rare)
  - 22 x Drow crossbows (fair quality) + 242 bolts
  - 22 x Drow rapiers of varying quality
  - 28 x Drow daggers of varying quality
  - 3 x Drake meat
  - 5 x Cured drake hide
  - 2 x Vials poisonous gas
  - 2 x Drake claws

Quest Log:

- **Main Quest - The RPG Awakening:**
  - Investigate the transformed world.
  - Level up.

- Do not die.
- Train your two disciples to become better warriors.

Leo grimaced as he read the upgrades to his Quests.

"Disciples," he groaned. "The System has a weird sense of fucking humor. Disciples my ass."

CHAPTER 9

They were ancient beyond human comprehension.

Six of them. One to watch over each Stat.

Strength (STR) - Gormrok the Titanlord
Dexterity (DEX) - Sylvaria, the Shadow Dancer
Constitution (CON) - Duragor, the Ironclad Sentinel
Intelligence (INT) - Aethralis, the Omniscient Archmage
Wisdom (WIS) - Circe, the Divine Oracle
Charisma (CHA) - Voxandra, the Enchanting Muse

They were beings of pure mana, but over the millennia they had taken on humanoid guises. An affectation as opposed to a necessity. And although they were not, strictly speaking - the System - they were ostensibly in charge of it.

To a point.

Circe waited for Gormrok, the final member of their cohort to arrive. She had already conjured up a round table with six throne-like chairs. In the center of the table, she had brought forth a crystal light that threw an orgy of colors across the room. Finally, a cornucopia of various foods. fruits, roast meats, breads, cakes, and fine wines.

Obviously, none of them actually needed material sustenance, but like their physical forms, it had become a lasting affection as well as an epicurean pleasure.

A ball of fluctuating blue and white light began to coalesce next to the table, and with a pop, Gormrok appeared.

He was an immense and towering deity that embodied raw physical power and indomitable strength. Clad in armor forged from the bones of ancient titans, Gormrok wielded a colossal warhammer that could shatter mountains with a single blow. His presence inspired awe, and his dominion over Strength ensured that those who sought his favor would gain unparalleled might on the battlefield.

He was also a bit of a dick.

"You are late," noted Circe.

"What is time but a false construct to guide the weak," replied Gormrok as he sat down, leaned forward, and drank a large swallow of wine straight from the bottle. Then he leaned to one side and let rip a thunderous fart.

"Ha, better out than in," he quipped.

"Why do you seek to embody the worst of the physical beings we emulate," sighed Voxandra, the enchanting muse of Charisma.

"Why not? Okay, Circe, why'd you call on us?" questioned Gormrok.

"Aethralis has picked up an anomaly on our latest Integration. Planet ERAZ."

Gormrok frowned. "Remind me."

Circe rolled her eyes. She knew that Gormrok was capable of recalling everything they had ever done, but his default setting was - be difficult. Nevertheless, she answered him. "Earth, Ragnaros, Aethera, and Zephyria, as I am sure you recall, Earth was of standard human stock, almost no mana. Ragnaros was multiple species, predominantly orcs, goblins, and trolls, with low mana. Aethera, elves, dwarves, fae, humanoid types, medium mana. And Zephyria, a planet so high in mana that nothing could live there. We used it to bolster the mana levels for the Integration of the other three planets. The new planet is called, ERAZ. As you already know."

Gormrok smirked. "Okay, so what's this anomaly?"

"It seems as though one of the Earth humans has taken on a pair of Disciples," answered Circe.

"So?" questioned Gormrok. "Why would that be a problem?"

"You know as well as I do," snapped Aethralis, the Omniscient Archmage in charge of Intelligence. "Every Integration is balanced on a knife's edge. The slightest miscalculation and we could end up with the opposite of what we set out to do. And not only has this human taken on Disciples, he is already above Level 50."

"Level 50 is nothing," said Gormrok. "I still don't see what you're getting your panties in a wad about," he continued.

Aethralis shook his head. "There is some truth in Gormrok's boorish comments. There is no guarantee that this anomaly will result in anything dire. However, what you do not seem to appreciate, is the human has gained these Levels in a matter of a few weeks."

"Impossible," scoffed Gormrok.

"Yet it has happened," stressed Aethralis.

"What are you saying?" asked Gormrok with a sneer. "Surely you don't think that…"

"We do," interjected Circe. "He is showing all of the signs. He might be – the One."

"Bullshit," scoffed Gormrock.

"All I'm suggesting is that we keep a close eye on him," said Circe.

Aethralis nodded. "I agree. I shall continue to study the patterns, and as soon as I have a more concrete idea, I shall contact you all."

"Don't bother," grunted Gormrok. "Storm in a teacup. Making mountains out of molehills you are."

"Perhaps," admitted Aethralis. "Perhaps not. But rather safe than sorry."

"Fair enough," conceded Circe. "Well, until we

meet again."

"I'm taking some of this wine," stated Gormrok. "Bloody waste of time. Cheers all, I'm outa here."

CHAPTER 10

Leo, Jane, and Bradley set up camp by a tranquil stream, surrounded by towering trees and fragrant scrub, providing a sense of security and tranquility.

As Leo kindled a fire, Jane and Bradley couldn't help but feel a profound sense of relief wash over them. The flickering flames seemed to chase away the lingering shadows of their past ordeal, replacing them with a warm glow of safety and camaraderie. With each crackle and pop of the firewood, their anxieties melted away, replaced by a newfound sense of security.

Jane found herself exhaling a breath, releasing a tension she hadn't realized she'd been holding since their harrowing escape from Conan's clutches, while Bradley's tense shoulders visibly relaxed as he settled down beside the fire.

Leo's confident demeanor and capable presence reassured them both, reminding them that they were no longer alone in their struggle against the chaos of the RPG apocalypse. As the fire grew brighter, casting its golden light over the campsite, Jane and Bradley exchanged grateful glances, silently acknowledging the unspoken bond that had formed between them and their newfound teacher, and protector.

As the flames danced in the firepit, casting a warm glow over the campsite, Leo took charge of the training session with a characteristic blend of authority and warmth. "Alright, folks," he began, his voice carrying a hint of playful camaraderie, "time to get down to business. We're gonna start with the basics, so don't worry if it feels a bit like mana manipulation 101." His words were met with nods of understanding from Jane and Bradley, their expressions a mix of anticipation and determination.

With a twinkle in his eye, Leo launched into the first lesson, guiding them through the fundamentals of meditation and mana sensing. "Alright, let's all take a deep breath and close our eyes," he instructed, his voice soothing yet firm. "Feel the energy of the forest around us, like a gentle breeze caressing your skin. Now, focus on your own mana, that inner spark of power within you." As they followed his instructions, Jane and Bradley felt a sense of calm wash over them, the worries of the day melting away in the serenity of the moment.

Leo's encouraging words spurred them on as they delved deeper into their training, his patience and guidance helping them navigate the intricacies of mana manipulation. "You're doing great, guys," he praised, his words a reassuring beacon in the darkness of uncertainty. "Just remember, it's all about practice and patience. Rome wasn't built in a day, and neither is mastery of mana."

As the evening unfolded and the training progressed, Leo couldn't help but feel a sense of pride swell within him as he witnessed Jane and Bradley's unexpected progress. "Looks like you two have been hiding some secret talents," he teased, a playful grin tugging at the corners of his lips. "Maybe I should've recruited you as my apprentices from the start."

"We're disciples," interjected Bradley. "Not apprentices."

"Fuck that," responded Leo. "I'm not some sort of religious leader, I'm just a simple dude who can manipulate mana."

Jane shot him a wry smile, her eyes sparkling with determination. "Who knew we had it in us, right?" she quipped, a hint of satisfaction evident in her tone.

Bradley nodded in agreement, a newfound confidence radiating from his demeanor. "I guess there's more to us than meets the eye," he mused, his voice tinged with a mix of surprise and excitement.

Leo chuckled at their banter, a sense of camaraderie settling over the campsite like a comforting blanket. "Well, don't let it get to your heads just yet," he teased, his tone lighthearted yet encouraging. "We've still got a long way to go before you're casting fireballs like a pro."

Despite the challenges ahead, Jane and Bradley couldn't help but feel a glimmer of excitement at the prospect of unlocking their potential under Leo's guidance. With each passing moment, they grew more confident in their abilities, buoyed by Leo's unwavering support and infectious enthusiasm. As the night wore on and the flames dwindled to embers, they knew that their journey was just beginning, but with Leo by their side, they were ready to face whatever challenges lay ahead.

"Right, that's enough for now," said Leo. "I could do with some chow. I wonder what drake steaks taste like?"

As the night deepened and the crackling flames danced higher, Leo's stomach rumbled in anticipation of the savory meal to come. He reached into his Inventory and retrieved some succulent drake steaks, the prized spoils of their recent battle.

With a flick of his wrist, Leo skewered the steaks onto sharpened lengths of wood, expertly arranging them over the fire. The scent of roasting meat mingled with the earthy aroma of the forest, creating an intoxicating bouquet that permeated the air around them.

Jane and Bradley watched with eager anticipation as the steaks sizzled and spat over the flames, their mouths watering at the prospect of a hearty meal after a long day of training. Leo couldn't help but smile at their enthusiasm, knowing that the simple pleasure of sharing a meal together would only strengthen their bond as a team.

As the steaks cooked to perfection, Leo's thoughts drifted to the challenges that lay ahead. But for now, in this moment of warmth and camaraderie, he found solace in the simple joys of good food and good company.

As the trio bit into their steaks, Leo nodded in satisfaction. "Could do with some salt and a beer, but it's surprisingly good."

"Thanks, boss," said Bradley "And not just for the cooking."

Leo grinned. He couldn't help but feel a sense of pride at Jane and Bradley's progress. "You know, you guys weren't bad for a couple of rookies," he remarked, a playful glint in his eye. "But don't go getting cocky just yet. Mastering mana manipulation is like learning to ride a horse. It takes time, patience, and a whole lot of falling off before you get the hang of it."

"Message received loud and clear, master," laughed Bradley.

"I'll *master* your ass," mumbled Leo.

Both Jane and Bradley chuckled at Leo's response.

With their bellies full and their spirits high, the trio settled in for the night, the crackling fire and twinkling stars serving as a comforting backdrop to their newfound camaraderie. As they drifted off to sleep, Leo couldn't help but feel a guarded sense of optimism for the journey ahead, happy in the fact that he was no longer alone.

CHAPTER 11

"Why haven't we come across any towns?" questioned Leo as they walked through the seemingly never-ending forest. "I mean, there used to be loads of small towns around the foothills. I'm talking human towns, not fucking elf treehouses, and Drow caves. Where the damn humans at?"

Leo and his two companions – sorry, disciples – had been walking east for three days now. They had come across two monsters, some sort of uber-leopard, Level 57, and a three-headed snake, Level 60.

They had dispatched them in a tidy fashion and both Bradley and Jane had gained a couple of levels and both were now on Level 7.

Leo had gained a single Level and had thrown his points into Strength again.

"I know, it's weird," agreed Jane. "I'm sure that some of the people died when the shit hit the fan, but we should have come across someone by now."

Leo stopped walking and took a deep breath.

"What?" asked Jane.

"*Some* people did not die," answered Leo.

"*Most* people died. Maybe ninety percent of the population. Maybe even more."

"Bullshit," said Bradley. "How would you know?"

"I just do," said Leo. "Trust me on this."

"My family," gasped Jane. "Are they all dead?"

"How should I know?" replied Leo. "Hopefully not. I'm assuming that my parents are still alive because if I didn't … look, let's just say, keep hope alive. Okay. Otherwise, it's just too fucking much to handle."

"Are you sure?" asked Jane. "About the numbers."

Leo nodded. "Sorry, I know it sucks. Fucking System."

They continued walking in silence, each lost in their own thoughts.

Every now and then, Leo would stop and use Identify on a plant, or bush, and if came up as something edible he would pick it, or dig it up and put it in his Inventory. "Getting a bit bored of just plain old drake steaks," he said. "Thought maybe some herbs, edible roots, and shit might break the monotony."

"Good idea," agreed Jane, and both she and Bradley joined in.

That night Leo cooked some steaks as usual, and to accompany them he roasted a few roots, similar to yams, in the fire. He had enough herbs and veggies to make some sort of stew, but as one of them had a pot, that idea was moot.

The next day the forest started to thin out, the trees smaller and less densely situated.

After an hour of walking, they spotted smoke. A couple of thin tendrils snaking upwards into the windless sky.

"Check it out," said Leo. "Looks like we might have found some civilization. I just hope they're human. Let's approach with caution, just in case."

It took the trio another half an hour to get close enough to the source of the smoke to see what it was.

"A village," said Jane. "And look, those guards at the gate. They're definitely human."

Leo frowned as he checked out the village. It was small, perhaps thirty buildings, surrounded by a six-foot-high wooden palisade wall. Two guards stood in the open gated entrance, both armed with roughly made spears. Leo used Identify and saw that both guards were Level 3 warriors. "This makes no sense," he said.

"What do you mean?" asked Bradley.

"The buildings, it's like they're all medieval. Where are the modern structures? If this was an existing town before, how come it's so fucking primitive. No street lights, thatched roofs, dirt streets."

"No idea," admitted Jane. "Why don't we just go there and ask them?"

"Okay, you guys stay behind me," said Leo. "Try to look harmless."

"I am harmless," countered Jane.

"True," agreed Leo. "But you know what I mean, don't look aggressive."

"Sure," answered Jane.

They approached the village, Leo in front, his two companions slightly behind him.

As soon as the guards caught sight of them, their spears were at the ready, a precaution in these uncertain times.

"Halt," commanded the first guard, his voice firm. "Who are you?"

Leo stepped forward; his demeanor calm yet wary. "Leo. This is Jane, and that's Bradley. We're sorta just wandering about, looking for civilization. We mean no harm."

The guards exchanged a glance, and then the first one nodded. "Step forward," he said, his tone slightly less hostile. "Slowly."

With cautious steps, the trio complied, their eyes scanning the surroundings for any signs of danger.

"So, can we come in?" Jane inquired, a note of curiosity in her voice.

The first guard turned to his companion, who shrugged. "I don't see why not," he said, a hint of resignation in his tone. "Tell you what, I'll take them to see the mayor." He turned to Leo. "My name's Peter, follow me."

"Tell me, Peter," Leo began, his voice tinged with curiosity. "What's the name of this place?"

"Penrose," Peter replied tersely, his gaze fixed ahead.

"Hey, I knew a Penrose," replied Leo. "Friend of mine lived there for a while before he moved to New York City. But that was quite a large place. Maybe four thousand people or so."

"Yeah," said the guard, his voice suddenly rough with emotion. "This is that same place. Part of the Canon City micropolitan area. Mind you, I heard that Canon City is no more. I mean, like, it just fucking vanished, along with the entire population."

"Hold on," interjected Leo. "How can this be the same Penrose? This is a medieval village, it's nothing like the town I knew."

"No shit," mumbled Peter. "One day we all woke up and this was it. Over three thousand five hundred people just weren't there no more. And the city had become this fucking pile of shit. Some people lost family, and we all lost friends. And since then, people are still dying. Monsters, sickness. It's like a never-ending nightmare."

"Man, I'm sorry to hear that," said Leo. Peter shrugged.

"Not your fault. It is what it is. Suppose I should be grateful I'm still alive. Anyway, here we are. The mayor's name is Tom Parry. Wait here, I'll call him." Peter knocked on the front door and then let himself in.

A minute later he returned and beckoned for them to come in. They followed him down a corridor and into a large office.

A man stood up from behind a desk and

walked over, hand outstretched. Leo shook it, as did Jane and Bradley. "Good day to you, folks, my name is Tom Parry, and I'm the mayor of Penrose. May I ask what you all doing here?"

"Good day, Mayor Parry," Leo greeted. "As I mentioned to your guards, we're looking for a place to stay for a short while, plus catch up on any information you might have for us"

Mayor Parry's gaze swept over the trio, his expression a mix of curiosity and concern. "I see," he murmured, his brow furrowing. "Well, you're certainly welcome here in Penrose. We may not have much to offer in terms of resources, but we do our best to support those in need."

Leo nodded appreciatively. "Thank you, Mayor Parry. We're grateful for your hospitality."

Jane and Bradley exchanged a glance, their relief palpable. Penrose seemed like a safe haven amidst the chaos of their journey, and they were eager to rest and regroup before continuing their travels.

Mayor Parry ushered them to seats, his demeanor friendly yet businesslike. "Please, make yourselves comfortable. Tell me more about your journey and how we can assist you."

Leo launched into an account of their travels and the challenges they faced. He didn't mention Mossweaver or his time in the tutorial Dungeon.

"In conclusion," said Leo. "We aren't looking to stay long, but any shelter would be appreciated. Being sleeping outdoors for a while now. Also, if I could purchase some basic cooking utensils, that would be great."

The mayor nodded. "I'll get Peter to sort you out. We have a few empty houses. And as far as pots and pans go, we have loads spare, so that shouldn't be a problem."

Ten minutes later, the trio found themselves in a simple, but clean two-room dwelling. There were a pair of beds a selection of blankets, and a sofa. A kitchen area with an open fire and a selection of pots, pans, and cutlery, a hand-operated water pump over a sink, and a small table with four chairs. On the table were a couple of candles.

"Shotgun one of the beds," said Leo.

"Shotgun the other one," announced Jane.

"Ah, shit," mumbled Bradley. "Looks like it's the sofa for me. Not that I'm complaining, still better than sleeping on the ground."

Leo pulled out some more drake steaks and the various root vegetables they had collected, and then he set about cooking a stew, pleased to find a carton of salt.

After they had eaten, they decided to have an early night, taking advantage of the fact they were sheltered and had something soft to lie on.

CHAPTER 12

Leo woke up with a start, an alarm ringing in his ears. It took him a few seconds to realize that the sound was internal and his screen showed a flashing red message.

Quest update – Protect the village of Penrose from three waves of beast attacks. The first attack will begin at sunrise, two days hence. Each successive attack will occur at twenty-four hours periods.

If you refuse this quest there will be consequences. Dire consequences. So, no backing out – get it?

"Shit," cussed Leo as he got out of bed.

Jane woke up. "What?" she mumbled.

"I just got a message from the System," replied Leo. "Apparently the village is going to be attacked by three consecutive monster waves. And I have been instructed to protect the town, or else."

"What you gonna do?"

"I'm going to get some advice," answered Leo.

"From who?"

"My mentor, master Mossweaver."

"Huh? Exclaimed Jane.

"Long story, I'll tell you later, right now I need to see if this ring works. Meanwhile, go wake Bradley up and tell him the news."

Jane nodded and left the room, heading to the sofa to shake Bradley awake.

Leo touched the ring and thought of Mossweaver. "Hey, master," he said. "Not sure how to do this. I need help."

There was a slight pause, and then Mossweaver's voice came to him. It sounded like he was talking from the bottom of a deep well, but Leo could still easily make out the words.

"Greetings, child, are you in danger?"

"No," replied Leo. "Well, not yet. But I got a message from the System telling me that the village I am currently in is going to be subjected to three waves of beast attacks. The first one starts in a couple of days. I was wondering if you had any advice."

"Yes," answered Mossweaver. "Leave the village as soon as possible. Wave attacks are not pleasant, and unless the village is well fortified and has a large contingent of high-level warriors, you will all most likely die."

"Can't leave," said Leo. "I was given a System-generated quest. And they were pretty fucking serious about the consequences if I don't do it."

Mossweaver sighed. "Okay," he said after he had paused to think. "You need to upgrade the village's defenses. I assume they have a wall."

"A wooden palisade. But there's only two days to prepare, so not sure what we can do."

"First, dig a series of trenches around the whole village. Try to get them at least four feet deep. Line the bottom with sharpened stakes. Then just before the wall, put more stakes. Bury them in the ground at a forty-five-degree angle facing outwards. Loads of them. If you still have any time left after that, do what you can to raise and strengthen the wall. Finally, make sure you organize the villagers into squads. Give each squad a set position. Archers, spearmen, healers, and so forth. And then pray to whatever gods you want, because this is going to be tough."

"Thank you, master," said Leo.

"Good luck, child."

Leo got up and left the cottage to speak to the mayor.

CHAPTER 13

Leo and Mayor Parry conferred in urgent whispers, their brows furrowed with concern. "We need to act fast," Leo urged, his voice low but urgent. Mayor Parry nodded solemnly, his eyes reflecting the gravity of the situation. Together, they hurried through the village streets, the distant clang of the alarm bell driving them forward.

As they reached the village center, the townsfolk began to emerge from their homes, drawn by the urgent call to action. Leo's heart raced as he surveyed the crowd, their faces a mixture of concern and determination. "Listen up, everyone," he called out, his voice cutting through the tense silence. "We've got a threat on our doorstep, and we need to prepare. The System has just informed me that Penrose is going to be attacked by three waves of beasts. The first one starting in two days. "

The villagers exchanged worried glances, but there was a sense of solidarity among them as they gathered around Leo. "What do we need to do?" one villager asked, their voice trembling with fear.

"We need to fortify our defenses," Leo replied, his tone firm and resolute. "We'll need teams to dig trenches and others to gather supplies for barricades. We can't let these monsters catch us off guard."

The villagers nodded in agreement, their expressions determined as they prepared for work. Leo moved among them, offering words of encouragement and guidance. "We can do this," he said, his voice unwavering. "Together, we'll make Penrose stronger than ever before."

Mayor Parry stepped forward, his voice firm as he addressed the crowd. "We're going to need everyone's help to get through this," he said, his words echoing off the surrounding buildings. "We'll need teams to dig trenches around the village, and others to strengthen our defenses. Let's work together and show these beasts that we won't go down without a fight."

The villagers nodded in agreement, their expressions grim but determined. With a sense of purpose, they divided into teams, some grabbing shovels and pickaxes while others began gathering materials for fortifications. The sounds of digging and hammering filled the air, accompanied by the occasional grunt of exertion.

Leo moved among the workers, offering guidance and encouragement as they worked to fortify their village. "Nice job, folks," he said, clapping a villager on the back as they laid the foundation for one of the trenches. "Keep up the good work, and we'll get through this together."

As the day wore on, the trenches began to take shape, their outlines becoming more defined with each passing hour. Sweat dripped from the brows of the villagers as they worked tirelessly to strengthen their defenses, their determination unwavering in the face of impending danger.

Leo directed teams of villagers to position sharpened stakes at the bottom of the trenches and along the walls, angled outward to ward off the approaching beasts. The sound of shovels scraping against the earth filled the air as the villagers worked tirelessly, driven by a sense of urgency.

"Make sure those stakes are nice and secure," Leo called out, his voice firm but encouraging. "We need to make these defenses impenetrable."

The villagers nodded in understanding, their expressions focused as they carried out Leo's instructions. "This is gonna keep us safe, right?" one villager asked, wiping sweat from their brow.

Leo flashed them a reassuring smile. "No worries, dude, I'm not going nowhere."

Leo distributed the crossbows, rapiers, and daggers from his Inventory to form squads among the villagers. The clinking of metal and the rustling of fabric filled the air as the villagers eagerly accepted their weapons, their faces a mix of determination and apprehension.

"Alright, folks, listen up," Leo called out, his voice projecting across the gathering. "We're gonna form squads to defend Penrose. Archers over there, spearmen, and swordsmen over here, and we'll need a few of you as stretcher bearers in case anyone gets injured."

The villagers nodded, some exchanging nervous glances as they prepared to take up their assigned positions. "Don't worry," Leo reassured them, "we've got this. Stick together, stay focused, and we'll get through this together."

Leo's high Charisma stat was working wonders with the villagers. Although many of them were showing obvious signs of fear, whenever Leo spoke, their faces lit up with trust, and hope.

Leo stood before the assembled villagers, his stance confident and authoritative. "Alright, everyone, listen up," he called out, his voice cutting through the quiet tension that hung in the air. "We don't have much time, so we need to make every moment count. I'm gonna teach you some basic combat maneuvers to help you defend yourselves and our village."

The villagers nodded eagerly, their eyes fixed on Leo as they awaited his instructions. "First things first," Leo began, gesturing for them to gather closer. "You need to know how to hold your weapons properly. Grip your swords firmly, but don't tense up too much. You want to be able to move quickly and fluidly."

As Leo demonstrated the proper grip and stance, the villagers followed suit, their movements hesitant at first but growing more confident with each repetition. "That's it," Leo encouraged them, a hint of pride in his voice. "Now, let's work on some basic strikes and parries."

The sounds of metal clashing filled the air as the villagers practiced their swordplay under Leo's guidance. Some stumbled and fumbled with their weapons, but Leo was patient, offering encouragement and advice to help them improve.

"We're gonna need to work together as a team," Leo explained, his gaze sweeping over the determined faces of the villagers. "Communication is key. If you see something, say something. We need to watch each other's backs out there."

The villagers nodded in agreement, their expressions resolute as they prepared to defend their home. With Leo's guidance, they practiced coordinating their movements and anticipating each other's actions, forging a sense of unity and purpose among them.

As the sun dipped below the horizon, casting long shadows across the village, the flickering torches came to life, bathing the gathered villagers in a warm, golden glow. Their faces were etched with determination, the firelight reflecting in their eyes as they listened intently to Leo's words.

"Listen up, everyone," Leo began, his voice ringing out strong and clear over the crackling of the flames. "Tomorrow, we face a great challenge. But I know that together, we are stronger than any foe we may encounter."

The villagers nodded in agreement, their expressions reflecting a mixture of fear and resolve. "We've worked hard to prepare for this moment," Leo continued, his tone filled with conviction. "We've dug trenches, laid traps, and armed ourselves with the weapons we need to defend our home. And tomorrow, we stand united against whatever may come our way."

A murmur of assent rippled through the crowd as Leo's words stirred something deep within them. They knew that the coming battle would not be easy, but they were ready to face it head-on, fueled by Leo's unwavering confidence and determination.

"Together, we will stand strong," Leo declared, his voice echoing with a sense of purpose. "We will not falter, we will not yield. We are the defenders of Penrose, and we will protect our home at all costs."

With a final rallying cry, Leo raised his fist in the air, the villagers joining him in a chorus of cheers and applause. In that moment, surrounded by the warmth of the fire and the strength of their community, they felt an unbreakable bond, ready to face whatever the next day may bring.

CHAPTER 14

As the first light of dawn broke over the horizon, the air was filled with tension and anticipation. Villagers clutched their weapons tightly, their eyes scanning the surrounding darkness for any sign of movement. The ground began to tremble, a low rumble echoing through the village as the first wave of beasts drew near.

"They're coming," someone whispered, their voice barely audible over the rising din of the approaching horde.

They came out of the forest, running at speed.

Leo used Identify on them.

"They're Iron Wolves," he yelled out. "Levels 10 to 20. Looks like there's only fifty or so. Come on guys, this shouldn't be a problem. Crossbows, wait, if they get past the first trench, hit them, but don't waste any ammunition yet."

The iron wolves were formidable-looking creatures, their massive frames towering over the villagers like dark shadows in the early morning light. Their fur was a deep, lustrous black, bristling with strength and vitality. Each wolf possessed eyes that gleamed with a primal hunger, their gaze piercing through the darkness with an unnerving intensity.

Sharp claws protruded from their massive paws, glinting in the sunlight as they slashed through the air with deadly precision. Long, razor-sharp teeth lined their jaws, ready to tear through flesh and bone with ease. Their growls reverberated through the air like thunder, sending shivers down the spines of even the bravest villagers.

As they charged forward, their movements were swift and sure, propelled by an insatiable hunger for blood and destruction. Each step shook the ground beneath them, a testament to their immense strength and ferocity.

The fastest members of the pack reached the first trench, some managed to jump over it. But Leo had instructed the villagers to mound the earth into a high berm on the opposite side of the trench, and the wolves that made it over hit the berm and fell backward into the trench.

Even though the wolves were tough and fast, they were also extremely heavy. And there were none higher than level 20. The sharpened wooden stakes were driven deep into them as they fell, killing some and badly wounding the rest.

More and more attempted to breach the trench but to no avail. The bodies began to pile up, some dead, some howling in pain as they tried to tear themselves off the stakes. Finally, in some parts of the trench, the bodies piled so high they filled the trench and formed a bridge across that allowed a large number of the wolves to get over.

"Ready, bowmen," yelled Leo. "Hold, aim, fire."

The crossbows fired almost as one, bolts thudding home, knocking some of the wolves from their feet. None died, but many were severely wounded.

And then Leo fired his bow.

The fully Imbued arrow streaked through the air and struck the leading wolf, exploding in a gout of flame and lightning. The explosion took out three more wolves and wounded many more.

The next arrow truck almost before the last explosion had subsided. Then another, and another.

This was simply too much for the remaining pack members and they finally broke and ran. Turning away from the village as they decided that discretion was now the better part of valor.

Leo continued to harass them as they retreated, firing three more arrows and killing another five of them.

Not one even made it to the second trench.

With the echoes of battle fading, the villagers and their newfound battle-leader, set to work amidst the lingering scent of sweat and blood.

Leo's voice rang out, directing the repair efforts with urgency. "Alright, folks, let's get these trenches cleared and those stakes replaced. We've got more work to do before nightfall."

Jane and Bradley joined in, their faces grim but determined as they lent their hands to the task at hand.

"Well, I guess we signed up for the whole 'fighting monsters' thing, huh?" Bradley quipped, a hint of nervousness in his voice as he hoisted a fallen stake into place.

Jane scoffed in disagreement, her expression a mixture of determination and apprehension. "Bullshit, the System volunteered us."

As they worked, the village buzzed with activity, the sound of shovels scraping against the earth mingling with the occasional clang of metal as stakes were hammered into place.

Leo's voice cut through the din, offering words of praise and encouragement to the weary villagers. "You all did an amazing job today," he declared, his tone filled with admiration. "But don't get too comfortable. Tomorrow will be even tougher, so we need to stay focused and ready for whatever comes our way."

The villagers nodded in agreement, their spirits bolstered by Leo's words. With renewed determination, they pressed on into the night, knowing that their efforts today were just the beginning of the battle to protect their home.

CHAPTER 15

The villagers gathered nervously at their designated positions, their eyes scanning the horizon for any sign of movement. The morning mist clung to the cobblestone streets, adding to the eerie atmosphere as the first light of dawn filtered through the trees.

The distant rumble of the approaching wave of monsters sent shivers down the spines of the villagers, and they tightened their grips on their weapons, readying themselves for battle. They all hoped against hope that they were not going to be faced with an unbeatable wave.

Leo stood tall at the forefront of the defenses, his brow furrowed in concentration as he surveyed the scene before him. The weight of responsibility hung heavy on his shoulders, but he showed no signs of wavering. Beside him, Bradley fidgeted nervously, his hands trembling ever so slightly as he conjured flames in anticipation of the coming onslaught.

The air was thick with tension, each passing moment punctuated by the sound of anxious murmurs and the occasional clang of metal as the villagers readied their weapons. The smell of smoke from the torches mixed with the earthy scent of the surrounding forest, creating a heady concoction that lingered in the air.

Despite the palpable fear that hung over the village, there was also a sense of determination and unity among the townsfolk. They knew that their survival depended on their ability to stand together and face the coming threat head-on. And as the sun continued its ascent into the sky, casting a warm glow over the village, they braced themselves for whatever lay ahead, ready to defend their home at all costs.

"Oh shit," breathed Leo as he saw the horde approaching. "Trolls and goblins. Here they come," Leo called out, his voice steady despite the tension in the air. "Get ready, everyone!"

The ground shook as the trolls lumbered forward, their massive forms casting menacing silhouettes against the rising sun.

"Don't panic," yelled Leo. "They're weak against fire!" Leo shouted to the gathered villagers. "Focus on the goblins. Leave the trolls to Bradley and me"

The villagers braced themselves as the horde drew nearer, their hearts pounding in their chests. The sight of the trolls' towering figures sent a ripple of fear through the crowd, but Leo's reassuring words helped to steady their nerves.

Bradley conjured flames in his palms, his face alight with determination as he prepared to unleash his magic against the approaching trolls.

"You heard the man!" he shouted to the villagers, a hint of nervous excitement in his voice. "Leave the big guys to us!"

The air was filled with the sounds of goblin spears clattering against their shields and the distant roar of the trolls as they hurled boulders toward the village walls.

Leo flashed Bradley a wry grin, his eyes twinkling with a mixture of adrenaline and dark humor. "Looks like we've got our work cut out for us, huh?" he quipped. "Just another day in paradise."

Bradley chuckled nervously, his shoulders tense with anticipation. "You know it," he replied, his voice strained but determined. "Let's show these SOB's what we're made of."

Meanwhile, the goblins surged forward, their shrill cries piercing the air as they charged towards the village. The first trench did little to deter them, as they laid long planks across it to create makeshift bridges. But the villagers had prepared well, and many goblins fell off the planks and met their end impaled on the sharpened stakes. The crossbowmen opened fire, bolts streaking through the air to hammer into the horde of green-skinned vermin.

Boulders slammed into the palisade, and some of the goblins began firing back, using the short bows. A couple of the villagers were hit, going down, yelling in pain.

The air filled with the clamor of battle as

the goblins rushed forward, their frenzied shouts mingling with the clash of weapons and the screams of the wounded. The scent of blood and sweat hung heavy in the air, adding to the sense of urgency that pervaded the battlefield.

"Keep firing!" shouted Leo, his voice cutting through the chaos as he directed the crossbowmen to unleash a volley of bolts at the oncoming horde. "We can't let them breach the defenses!"

Jane rushed forward to assist the wounded, her brow furrowed with concentration as she applied bandages and administered healing spells. "Hang in there," she whispered to a villager, her voice a reassuring presence amidst the chaos. "You're going to be okay."

Bradley's flames illuminated the battlefield, casting flickering shadows as he hurled fireballs toward the trolls. "Eat fire, you ugly shitty crap-faced douches," he yelled, his voice tinged with exhilaration as he watched the trolls stumble and roar in pain.

Leo couldn't help but grin at Bradley's strange way of cussing. Then he wound up a massive fireball and unleashed it. The flaming ball careened across the battlefield, crashing into one of the trolls and exploding, taking out a raft of goblins with it. The troll keened in agony as the fire flayed the flesh from his bones.

The crossbowmen continued to fire, although they were now dangerously low on ammunition. Their bolts were cutting down scores of goblins with each volley. Yet, despite their efforts, the sheer number of attackers meant that some managed to breach the second trench and scramble over the walls.

The village spearmen fought valiantly, their weapons flashing in the fading light as they stabbed down at the climbing goblins.

But it was Leo who truly turned the tide, leaping from the walls with a roar of defiance and wading into the fray with his axe.

"Keep fighting!" Leo's voice rang out above the din, his words a rallying cry for the defenders as he charged headlong into the fray. His axe gleamed in the fading light, each swing a deadly dance of steel as he cut down goblins with ruthless precision.

Bradley's fireballs exploded amidst the goblin ranks, sending flames licking at their heels and driving them back with a fierce intensity. "Feel the burn, you green pieces of shit," he shouted, his voice filled with determination as he unleashed another volley of flames.

The clash of metal against metal echoed through the village as Leo, a towering figure amidst the chaos, wielded his mana-imbued axe with lethal precision. His movements were fluid yet powerful, each swing slicing through the air with a menacing whoosh.

Sweat beaded on Leo's brow as he fought, his muscles straining with the effort of each blow. But there was a determination in his eyes, a fierce resolve that burned bright even amidst the chaos of battle.

The scent of blood and smoke hung heavy in the air. It was a cacophony of senses, each sound and smell adding to the intensity of the moment.

With each swing of his axe, Leo cleaved through the goblin ranks, his movements a deadly dance of steel and sinew. He moved with an agility and grace that belied his size, his every action calculated and precise.

Finally, the goblins began to falter, their ranks thinning under Leo's relentless assault. With a triumphant roar, he pressed the attack, driving the vermin back until they were forced to retreat in disarray.

Leo stood still, taking in deep breaths as he waited for his remarkable Constitution to heal the myriad of wounds that covered his face and body, drenched in blood, both his and the enemy's.

He could hear the villagers cheering, chanting his name, and yelling out in sheer jubilation. The joy of winning, the joy of surviving.

The relief of being not dead.

With the battle won, the village of Preston breathed a collective sigh of relief, though the toll of the fight weighed heavily on their hearts. Two fallen comrades were mourned, their absence a somber reminder of the cost of victory. Around them, wounded villagers groaned in pain, their injuries a stark testament to the brutality of the battle.

Jane moved among the wounded, her healing

magic offering solace to those in need. With gentle words and soothing touches, she worked tirelessly to ease their suffering, her presence a beacon of hope amidst the aftermath of chaos.

Meanwhile, Leo wasted no time in rallying the villagers to action once more. With a sense of grim determination, he directed them in the grim task of cleaning up the battlefield. The air was thick with the stench of blood and sweat, a grim reminder of the violence that had unfolded just moments before.

Amidst the sounds of shovels scraping against the earth and the clatter of discarded weapons, Leo's voice rang out, firm and authoritative. "We must fortify our defenses," he declared, his words a call to action. "More beasts will come at first light tomorrow, and we must be ready."

With renewed purpose, the villagers set to work, clearing away the fallen and reinforcing the defenses of their village. Stakes were reset, trenches were dug deeper, and crossbow bolts were collected for reuse. It was a grim task, but one that they undertook with a quiet determination, knowing that their survival depended on it.

As the sun dipped below the horizon, casting long shadows across the village, the work continued unabated. Though weary and bruised, the villagers pressed on, their spirits bolstered by the knowledge that they had faced the darkness and emerged victorious.

CHAPTER 16

The morning mist swirled thickly across the landscape, making it difficult to see beyond a hundred yards. As the sun rose over the trees, it appeared blood red and uninspiring, almost as if it was just fulfilling an obligation rather than being genuinely interested.

Leo stood at the wall, waiting patiently. His sense of mana had alerted him about an incoming wave, but as it drew nearer, he was taken aback to see that it wasn't a swarm of creatures. Instead, there was only one creature, which was extremely enormous.

The air was filled with a sense of anticipation as the ground shook under the weight of approaching footsteps. Villagers peered anxiously over the walls, their hearts pounding with fear as they tried to catch a glimpse of the approaching mob in the thick mist.

As they gazed into the distance, they noticed something looming. It was a colossal Cyclops heading towards their village. With every heavy step, the ground shook and the air filled with the sound of creaking armor and strained metal. The

Cyclops was over 40 feet tall, towering above the village like a massive mountain of muscle and sinew. Its weapon, a club larger than a tree, was raised high, poised to cause destruction upon the unsuspecting villagers.

The armor of the Cyclops was a chaotic amalgamation of mismatched pieces, a collection of salvaged metal scraps that produced a clanking and rattling sound with each movement.

A palpable stench of decay and sweat emanated from the creature like a miasma, a foul odor that hung heavily in the air and sent shivers down the spines of those unfortunate enough to catch its scent.

For most of the villagers, the foul smell triggered a primal instinct to flee, their bodies recoiling in fear at the mere presence of the monstrous Cyclops.

However, amidst the chaos and panic, Leo remained steadfast, his senses unaffected by the Cyclops's aura of fear due to his incredibly high Wisdom and Intelligence stats. With a calm demeanor and steely resolve, he assessed the situation, his mind clear and focused despite the looming threat.

While others faltered in the face of danger, Leo stood tall.

Using Identify, he tried to get as much info as he could about the approaching monster.

Giant Cyclops - (Level 99)

Strengths –

Immense size and strength: The Cyclops possesses unparalleled physical power, capable of wielding its massive club with devastating force. Its sheer size allows it to overpower most opponents with ease, crushing anything in its path.

Fear-inducing presence: The Cyclops's imposing stature, mind-altering stench, and ferocious demeanor instill fear in all who behold it, sowing panic and confusion among its enemies. Its mere presence can demoralize even the bravest of warriors, leaving them vulnerable to its onslaught.

Weaknesses –

Lack of agility: Despite its formidable strength, the Cyclops is slow and cumbersome, hampered by its massive size and unwieldy movements. Its lack of agility makes it vulnerable to swift and nimble opponents who can evade its attacks with ease.

Single eye: The Cyclops's single eye, while granting it enhanced depth perception and keen sight, also presents a significant weakness. Blinding or incapacitating its eye can greatly impair its ability to perceive and engage its enemies, leaving it vulnerable to attack.

Vulnerability to ranged attacks: While formidable in close combat, the Cyclops is susceptible to attacks from a distance. Its size and slow movement make it an easy target for ranged weapons such as bows and crossbows, allowing foes to weaken it from afar before engaging in melee combat.

Limited intelligence: Like many giant creatures, the Cyclops is often portrayed as lacking in intelligence, relying more on brute strength than cunning strategy. Its limited intellect can be exploited by clever adversaries who can outmaneuver it with tactics and trickery.

"Holy moly," murmured Leo. "Level 99. You gotta be shitting me."

As the Cyclops drew nearer, Leo addressed the villagers, his voice steady and reassuring amid the clamor of fear and uncertainty. "Stay strong, my friends," he said, his words a beacon of hope in the darkness. "We can ice this huge fucker together, but we gotta stand united. Ignore the fear. Remember, you dudes are fighting for your homes, your family, your friends."

Leo leaned as hard as he could into his Charisma stat, doing his best to exude an aura of steadfast bravery and belief to all those around him.

"As soon as that ugly bastard is in range, I want

you crossbowmen to attack. Aim for its eye. The dick head has only got one, so we take that out and it might even things up a little."

With Leo's leadership, the villagers found renewed courage, their fear giving way to determination as they prepared to face the Cyclops head-on. Armed with weapons and resolve, they stood ready to defend their home against the monstrous invader, their hearts filled with the hope of victory against impossible odds.

Leo stood firm, his heart pounding in his chest as he faced down the colossal Cyclops. With a defiant roar, he notched an arrow onto his bow, the familiar weight of his soul-bound Bow of Storms comforting in his hands. As he drew back the string, channeling mana into the arrow, he focused on the towering beast before him.

Leo's arrow cut through the air with great speed and energy, heading straight towards the Cyclops. However, the monster seemed to be unaware of the danger, as it was focused on the village that lay beyond.

Standing next to Leo, Bradley began hurling fireballs at the Cyclops, causing flames to lick at the monster's feet. Despite this, the Cyclops continued to move forward, seemingly unfazed by the attacks.

Encouraged by Leo's words, the villagers joined the fight, firing their crossbows at the Cyclops. However, despite its size, the Cyclops' single eye was relatively small and difficult to hit. Even Leo struggled to hit the target, let alone the amateur crossbowmen.

As the Cyclops drew closer, its monstrous form casting a shadow over the battlefield, Leo knew they had to act fast. With a swift motion, he stowed his bow and summoned forth his mana, gathering it into a potent bolt of energy. With a mighty heave, he hurled the mana bolt toward the Cyclops's head. Then he immediately launched another and another. A volley of mana bolts screamed and crackled toward the Cyclops.

Some of the mana bolts almost found their mark, striking the Cyclops's forehead with explosive force. But for every hit, there were countless more that complexly missed the monster. The creature's relentless advance was bringing it ever closer to the village's defenses.

With each thunderous footfall, the ground trembled beneath their feet, a stark reminder of the imminent danger they faced. Roaring in rage, the Cyclops used its massive club to brush the sharpened stakes aside, then it simply stepped over the first trench with contemptuous ease.

As the Cyclops approached, its massive body casting a terrifying shadow over the village, Leo understood that he needed to take drastic action. He equipped his spear, feeling the reassuring weight of the weapon in his hands. Without a moment's hesitation, he jumped from the safety of the wall and charged towards the giant creature, his heart pounding in his chest.

The air was thick with tension as Leo faced off against the mighty Cyclops. In a blur of lightning-fast strikes and nimble dodges, he danced around his towering opponent, his spear poised for the perfect moment to strike. And then, with a fierce battle cry, he charged forward with all his might, aiming straight for the Cyclops' Achilles tendons. The sound of metal clashing against flesh thundered through the village, drowning out everything else in a symphony of pure, adrenaline-fueled battle.

Sweat beaded on Leo's brow as he danced around the massive creature, his muscles straining with each movement.

"Good lord, but this dude is ripe," mumbled Leo to himself as the monster's incredible stench bore down on him like a weight.

As Bradley stood safely behind the wall, he shouted, "You're a beast, boss! Keep pushing!"

With her heart racing faster than ever, Jane cheered loudly, "You're crushing it, Leo! Don't you dare slow down now!"

Leo's spear finally found its mark, slicing through the Cyclops' thick tendon. He was about to revel in his victory, but before he could catch his breath, the giant's massive club, as thick as a tree trunk, struck Leo's shoulder with a bone-crushing force. The battle had just reached a whole new level of intensity!

The blow smashed Leo off his feet and sent him tumbling across the ground until he cracked up against the village palisade. He struck the wall with such force it dented his armor, and the sound of his ribs breaking was clearly audible.

"Leo," shouted Jane. "Someone, help me get to him."

One of the villagers ran up with a length of rope that he tied to one of the logs that formed the wall. Jane clambered down, slipping halfway down, falling to the ground, and twisting her knee. Ignoring the pain, she hobbled over to Leo's prostrate body and knelt beside him.

Laying her hands on him, she poured her healing mana into him.

Meanwhile, every crossbowman opened up on the Cyclops. Some villagers even threw stones, sticks, and flaming torches. Anything to take the monster's attention off their fallen warrior.

Leo was in a bad way. In fact, if he hadn't invested so many points into Constitution there would have been no chance of him surviving that massive hit. As it was, Jane could tell, via her Healing skill, that all of his ribs were broken, two of them had penetrated his lungs, his left arm and shoulder were shattered, and he had internal bleeding.

He was also unconscious.

"Come on, Leo," urged Jane as she continued her Healing. She could hear the ribs and bones grinding together as she poured more mana into him, and then his shoulder popped and she could sense his lungs healing up.

As she toiled away, her heart racing with fear, the Cyclops drew closer. Suddenly, a brave villager leaped from the wall, brandishing a sharp spear. With a fierce battle cry, he charged toward the monstrous beast, skillfully dodging a blow from its massive club. Striking with all his might, he aimed for the wound that Leo had already inflicted on the Cyclops' right Achilles tendon. Though the strike barely made a dent, it did grab the monster's attention, causing it to slam its unwieldy club on the ground in an attempt to crush its daring new attacker.

Leo's eyes finally flickered open and he stared at Jane for a few seconds before he spoke.

"Hey, what's a nice girl like you doing in a place like this?"

"Asshole," replied Jane. "I thought you were dead."

"It'll take more than a forty-foot-tall monster wielding a fucking tree to kill me," quipped Leo. "Thanks for the save. I owe you."

He turned to see the lone spearman harassing the Cyclops. "Now that dude has massive cojones," commented Leo. "Look at him go. Better go help the guy out."

Leo's eyes burned with determination as he conjured up a massive fireball, ready to take down the Cyclops. With a fierce battle cry, he launched the fireball straight at the monster's face, blinding it and leaving its flesh deeply scorched. Seeing his chance, Leo sprinted forward with lightning-fast speed, his Stats making him a blur to anyone watching.

Equipping his trusty axe, he used his momentum to deliver a powerful blow to the monster's Achilles tendon, severing it completely. The ground shook with the force of the impact as the Cyclops stumbled, roaring in pain. Leo knew he had the upper hand now, and he wasn't about to let this opportunity slip away.

With a deafening bellow, the Cyclops stumbled to one knee, clutching its face in agony. Leo seized the moment and quickly conjured a massive ball of crackling mana, ready to strike. Without hesitation, he charged towards the wounded giant, took aim and hurled the bolt with all his might. The electric blast whizzed through the air, striking the monster's lone eye with a thunderous explosion that burst it like a grotesque water balloon.

The villagers were encouraged by Leo's bravery and decided to unite to face the Cyclops head-on. They flung open the gates of the village and joined the fight alongside Leo and the lone spearman. The air was filled with the twang of bowstrings and the clash of swords as they fought with all their might, pouring their heart and soul into every strike. Together, they pushed back against the ferocious beast, determined to emerge victorious.

The ground shook as the Cyclops swung its massive club, unleashing chaos among the determined villagers. But they refused to back down, launching an all-out assault on the beast with arrows, swords, axes, and fists.

The battle raged on, and the air was thick with the sound of clashing metal and the scent of blood.

The villagers fought bravely, but the monster was relentless, striking down three of them with brutal force. Jane, however, refused to give up. She rushed to their aid, desperately trying to save them. In the end, she managed to rescue one of them, but the other two were beyond her reach.

It was a fierce fight, but the villagers had proven that they were not to be underestimated.

During the intense battle, the villagers fought bravely and with great determination, seeking to overcome their fear and frustration by taking it out on the fallen beast. The air was thick with the scent of earth, sweat, and adrenaline as they fought the monstrous Cyclops, with each moment feeling like an eternity. Their hearts pounded with a mix of emotions as they fought on with unwavering courage.

Leo figured that he could have taken the Cyclops out by himself, now it was blind and crippled, but he knew that the villagers needed this. They needed to be involved in the monster's final demise.

They had suffered casualties, but it would bolster their confidence in the days to come. They would remember the moment, remember that they were not helpless.

They were warriors.

"We're doing it! Keep fighting!" Leo encouraged, his voice ringing out amidst the din of battle.

And finally, with a final, decisive blow, they brought the Cyclops crashing down to the ground, defeated.

A celebratory chorus of triumph rang out through the village, as they rejoiced in their hard-earned victory, united in their resilience and courage.

CHAPTER 17

It had been a couple of hours since they had dispatched the Cyclops. Leo had helped clear up, and he had looted the monster, getting a sharp tooth, a section of cured hide, and a large amount of gold coins. He added that to the loot he had collected from the first two waves. Five Iron Wolf pelts, some claws, and a few goblin bows and spears. He could have taken more, but he let the villagers claim the lion's share of the spoils. In fact, he had given them everything except the Iron Wolf pelts, figuring he could always get more loot. He also let them keep the Dark Elf weaponry he had distributed before the monster waves.

He had no idea what he was going to do with his loot, but he hoped he would come across some System-run shop where he could sell it. That is, if they existed.

Mind you, that would just get him yet more gold, and up to now, he had not found a place where he could actually spend any of it.

He pulled up his Stat sheet to check out how many levels he had gained, and to allocate his points. He had jumped up 4 Levels, and having come so close to death, again, he chucked the 20 points into Constitution.

He noticed that he had gained another two official titles – **Warrior Lord** and **Cyclops Slayer**.

"Warrior Lord," he mumbled to himself. "What the fuck does that mean?"

He glanced through the rest of the sheet to see what other gains he had made.

Character Name: Leo Armstrong (Human)

Class: *Stormcaller Archmage-Hunter*

Titles: Friend of the Elves
Warrior Lord
Cyclops Slayer

Level: 62

Experience Points (XP): 8200000/9000000

Stats:
- **Strength (STR):** 554
- **Dexterity (DEX):** 504
- **Constitution (CON):** 854
- **Intelligence (INT):** 504
- **Wisdom (WIS):** 594
- **Charisma (CHA):** 453

Stat points available - 0

Note - 5 Stat points are made available during each Level gained.

Skills:

- **Axe Throwing (Level 12):** subject is skilled in throwing axes accurately, dealing damage from a distance.
- **Survival (Level 15):** subject can navigate through wilderness, track animals, and find resources efficiently.
- **Archery (Level 25):** subject is proficient with a bow, allowing him to shoot arrows with power and accuracy.
- **Camping (Level 6):** subject excels at setting up camps, building fires, and surviving in outdoor environments.
- **Cooking (Level 5):** The subject can prepare simple and nutritious meals using outdoor ingredients.
- **Axe Wielding (Level 30):** subject can wield an axe with a good degree of proficiency.
- **Lighting Infusion (Level 18):** subject can infuse his arrows with the power of a Thunderbolt.

Wind Infusion (Level 20): subject can infuse his arrows with the power of the Wind, this allows the arrow to travel further, faster and with more accuracy.

Spear Wielding (Level 18): subject is now proficient in spear combat.

Mana Manipulation & Core Control (Level 36): subject can now actively affect external mana.

Dagger Wielding (Level 4): subject can now use his dagger to deal death.

Inventory:

- **Weapons:**
  - Throwing Axes (x2)
  - Battle Axe
  - Bowie Knife
  - Bow of Storms (Soulbound)
  - Quiver of Antiquity (Soulbound)
  - Starforged Spear (Soulbound)

- **Armor:**
  - Leather tunic with metal scales (Self-repairing, self-cleaning)
  - Vambrace (x2) (Self-repairing, self-cleaning)
  - Reinforced Leather Boots (Self-repairing, self-cleaning)
  - Stout leather trousers with metal scales (Self-repairing, self-cleaning)

- **Consumables:**
  - Healing Potion (5)
  - Rations (3 days)

- **Tools:**
  - Flint and Steel
  - Compass
  - Climbing Gear

- **Miscellaneous:**
  - Map of the RPG Earth
  - 720 gold coins

- Verdant Moonlight Amulet (Rare)
- 5 x Iron Wolf pelts
- 2 x Drake meat
- 5 x Cured drake hide
- 2 x Vials poisonous gas
- 2 x Drake claws

Quest Log:

- **Main Quest - The RPG Awakening:**
- Investigate the transformed world.
- Level up.
- Do not die.
- Train your three disciples to become better warriors.

"Hold on," he said out loud. "What the actual fuck? *Three* disciples. Why *three*?"

Before he could give it some thought, a man approached.

"My lord," he greeted Leo.

Leo turned to look at him. "Hey, I know you. You're the spear dude with massive steel balls. I owe you one, my man. You may very well have saved my life, attacking that Cyclops like a fucking psycho. Nice one. What can I do you for?"

"I've just been talking to Janet and Bradley…" The man hesitated.

"Talk to me, dude," urged Leo. "Hold on, I can't just keep calling you, dude. What's your name?"

"Buck Johnson. Level 9 Warrior, got some spear skills, plus shield skills."

"Okay, Buck, as I said, talk to me."

"I want to become a disciple," said Buck, his eyes brimming with enthusiasm.

"Oh, fuck me," murmured Leo. "So that's what the System was on about. Look, Buck, seriously, this whole disciple thing makes me very uncomfortable. It's not like I'm some kinda religious leader. I'm just a dude who can do some stuff better than most humans at the moment."

"I understand," said Buck. "So, is that a yes or a no, my lord?"

"Don't call me, lord," snapped Leo. "And I suppose the answer has to be yes because the fucking System has basically snookered me."

Buck took a knee. "Thank you, my lord."

Leo shook his head. "Oh, for fucks sake."

***

"He has taken on another disciple," noted Circe, the divine oracle of Wisdom. "That is interesting."

"I agree," responded Aethralis, the omniscient Archmage of Intelligence. "This is more than a trend, it is a direction."

"Should we tell the others?" asked Circe.

Aethralis nodded. "Except for Gormrok. There would be no pint. He would simply fart, say something insulting and tell us to stop acting like a bunch of old women."

Circe laughed, the sound like a musical stream, full of joy and happiness, a result of her infinite Level Charisma. "I agree, I will inform the others.

This is most definitely getting interesting; I shall continue to keep a close eye on things."

"As will I," concurred Aethralis as he teleported away in a blaze of mana.

CHAPTER 18

As the sun rose over the trees, Leo stood opposite his three companions ... oops, disciples.

Jane, Bradley, and Buck stood in a row. They had all assumed the position – legs shoulder width apart, knees slightly bent, palms of their hands on their thighs.

Meditating.

Leo was teaching them how to access their mana. He had already done this a few times with Jane and Bradley and was pleased with the results. However, Buck had caught up with the other two extremely quickly. He was an exemplary student.

After chatting with him, Leo learned why. Before the apocalypse, Buck had been a martial arts trainer. Specifically, Adimurai. An Indian martial art developed in Kanyakumari, an Indian province in the southernmost region of the country. And as such, he was well-schooled in both combat and meditation.

During the battle for Penrose, both Jane and Bradley had gained a few levels and had been awarded their upgraded classes.

Jane was now Level 11, and her new class had been upgraded from Healer to **Life Warden**. This came with higher healing, and because it was now no longer only a dedicated Healing class, it boasted an offensive spell as well, Holy Mana Bolt.

Bradley was Level 10, and his class had progressed from Fire Mage to **Flame Sovereign**. This class gave him the ability to launch streams of flame as well as fireballs.

When he had found that out, he had literally danced a jig and called himself, a human flame-thrower.

Leo was not concerned about being attacked or surprised in any way, because his mana awareness had reached a level where he could sense all living things within a two-mile radius, further if he really put some effort into it.

He let his mana awareness roam, pushing it out in different specific directions to see how far he could reach.

And then he felt it. Some three miles away. A hint of life, human, but barely there. It was the aura of a person in pain. A person clinging to life by a thread.

"Guys," said Leo. "That's enough, we got someone in trouble. About three miles away. Follow me."

Guided by a sense of urgency, Leo and his companions sprang into action, their feet pounding against the forest floor with determination. The thick foliage surrounded them, casting shifting shadows as they darted through the trees, their senses heightened by the urgency of their mission.

Leo held himself back so he didn't outstrip his companions. Because even though they were all now faster than any Olympic athlete, they weren't even close to approaching the superhuman speed that Leo could.

As they ran, the atmosphere was tense and heavy. The only sounds were the rustling of leaves and the rhythmic beat of their footsteps. The air was filled with the aroma of pine needles, which mixed with the faint scent of smoke in the distance. This was a somber reminder of the danger they might be rushing to confront.

"We're getting close," Leo murmured, his voice barely above a whisper. "Stay focused, everyone. Whoever it is, they are barely alive."

After a tense journey through the dense forest, Leo and his companions finally emerged into a small clearing where the village stood. However, what they saw was a scene of utter devastation. The once-sturdy wooden wall that encircled the village lay in ruins, with splintered beams scattered haphazardly across the ground. The charred remains of buildings were still smoldering in the aftermath of a fierce blaze, which was sending plumes of acrid smoke drifting into the air.

The scene was hauntingly silent, save for the crackling of flames and the occasional creak of charred wood settling. The air was heavy with the scent of smoke, stinging their nostrils and causing tears to well up in their eyes. The sense of desolation weighed heavily upon them as they surveyed the destruction before them.

As Leo gazed upon the ruined village, his heart clenched with sorrow at the sight of what had once been a bustling community. The devastation was overwhelming, and he couldn't help but imagine the suffering of the inhabitants.

Leo pointed towards the far end of the village. "The person we are looking for is that way," he said with a grim expression.

With a sense of determination, they pressed forward into the village. Every step they took felt like a solemn march through a graveyard. The once-paved streets were now littered with debris and rubble, and the sounds of their footfalls mingled with the eerie silence that surrounded them. They kept their senses alert for any sign of life amidst the devastation, hoping to find some survivors.

As they moved deeper into the village, Leo couldn't help but feel a pang of empathy for the people who had once called this place home. The carcasses of their homes and businesses were a stark reminder of the fragility of life and the importance of cherishing the time we have with our loved ones.

The team's footsteps echoed hollowly against the ground as they made their way through the ruins, their hearts heavy with sorrow at the sight of the devastation. The lifeless bodies of villagers lay scattered amidst the wreckage, their limbs twisted at unnatural angles and their faces frozen in expressions of fear and anguish.

Some were bearing signs of brutal dismemberment. The sight sent a shiver down their spines, the horror of the massacre weighing heavily on their hearts.

In the midst of the wreckage, a faint whimper caught their attention, drawing their gaze toward a figure lying motionless on the ground.

"There she is," yelled Leo, and they all ran towards her.

The young woman's frail form was barely visible amidst the debris, her shallow breaths barely stirring the air around her. With a sense of urgency, Jane hurried to her side, her hands glowing with healing energy as she worked to revive the girl.

"I've got you," Jane murmured softly, her voice a comforting presence amidst the chaos.

Leo knelt beside them, his expression grave as he handed Jane a Healing Potion from his inventory. "Here, this should help," he said, his tone reassuring as he watched Jane's efforts. Jane tipped the girl's head back and dribbled the red liquid into her mouth, the potion aiding Jane's already potent healing powers.

Slowly, the woman's eyes fluttered open, revealing a glimmer of consciousness amidst the chaos surrounding them. Her gaze met theirs, gratitude shining in her weary eyes as she struggled to sit up.

"Thank you," she whispered, her voice trembling with emotion as she looked at Leo and his companions. "I don't know what I would have done without your help. I thought I was dead. Who are you? Where is everyone else?"

"My name is Leo. This is Jane, our Healer. Bradley and Buck. As to where everyone else is … I'm real sorry, but so far, we haven't seen any other survivors. What happened here?"

"Fucking System," sighed the woman as she collected herself before sharing the horrific events that had occurred in her village.

In vivid detail, she recounted the harrowing incident where they were mercilessly attacked by the formidable and intimidating Humanoid Fortis'. These towering beasts were heavily muscled, and their imposing presence alone was enough to instill fear in the hearts of anyone who crossed their path. The attack was sudden and vicious, with the creatures displaying a brutal ferocity that left them with no chance to defend themselves.

The memories flooded back for Leo, bringing him back to the early days of the RPG apocalypse when he had first encountered these formidable foes.

"Yeah, I know those fuckers," said Leo. "How many of them?"

The woman shook her head. "Not sure. Loads."

"Sorry, I should have asked sooner," said Leo. "What's your name?"

"Lyra Blackthorne," she answered. "Level 8 Rogue."

"Well, Lyra, let's get out of this graveyard and set up camp a couple of miles away. Then we'll figure on what to do next."

Lyra nodded and stood up, ready to follow her saviors.

CHAPTER 19

"So what you're telling is, a bunch of adventurers from you village went out to do some grinding, and they came across some sort of scroll that had a map to a Lost City?"

Lyra nodded. "Actually, it wasn't a map, as such. But it did contain directions, clues, that sort of thing. It spoke of a hidden temple deep within the forest, rumored to contain relics of immense power left behind by an ancient civilization. Which is strange, because isn't this world like only a few months old? Don't see how it can have the remains of an ancient race."

"Okay, I get it," noted Leo. "But what I don't get is what this has to do with the Gorilla Goons attacking your village."

"Gorilla Goons?" questioned Jane.

Leo shrugged. "Easier to say than Humanoid Fortis."

"Jeez, barely."

"Okay, what do you suggest? I'm not gonna call them those asswipes by their System-approved moniker. Fuck that."

"I had a British boyfriend once," continued Jane. "When he wanted to insult someone, he used to call them a Pillock. Not sure what it means."

"Fine," sighed Leo as he turned back to Lyra. "What I don't get is what this has to do with those Pillocks attacking your village."

"I don't know for sure," replied Lyra. "But all I can assume is that somehow, they knew that we had the scroll. Maybe they followed the team back, who knows? All I do know is that they attacked at dawn, trashed the wall, and demanded we hand over the scroll. Our chief, Barton Dovecote, decided that we didn't stand a chance against them, so he did as they demanded and handed the scroll over."

Lyra took a deep shuddering breath as she tried to control her emotions. "They took the scroll, and then proceeded to attack the village, burning, killing." Lyra let out an involuntary sob. "It was a massacre."

Jane put her arm around the young woman as she continued to cry.

No one spoke for a while. What could they say? Lyra had just lost everyone she ever knew.

When she had stopped crying, Leo leaned towards her. "Do you have any idea where these Pillocks live?"

She nodded and pointed west. "About fifteen miles that way. I don't know exactly, I just remember some of our scouts talking about it. Why?"

"I reckon we should pay them a visit. Just take a closer look."

"Apparently, there's like five hundred of them," said Lyra. "And they're really dangerous."

Leo smiled ominously. "Yeah, so am I."

***

As Leo and his companions ventured deeper into the woods, the sun filtered through the thick canopy above, casting dappled shadows on the forest floor. The air was cool and damp, carrying with it the earthy scent of moss and fallen leaves. In the distance, birds chirped, their melodic songs adding to the tranquil atmosphere.

In contrast, every now and then they would hear the raucous screech of some sort of large, flying raptor, or the roar of a forest beast. But Leo's mana awareness kept them away from the myriad of predators.

As they trudged through the trees, the tension among the group was palpable. Each step brought them closer to their destination, yet uncertainty loomed like a dark cloud overhead.

Leo had gone into his Status sheet, and after some digging found how to link them all together as a party. He had done that at Bradley's suggestion. Both Bradley and Jane were keen gamers back before the world got fucked up. Leo had gamed, but not at the level the other two did. He had no idea where Buck and Lyra stood on the issue, and he reminded himself to talk about it at a later stage.

Jane glanced nervously at the dense underbrush, her senses heightened as she scanned the surroundings for any signs of danger.

Bradley walked with a determined stride, his jaw set in a firm line as he gripped his staff tightly.

Buck's eyes darted from tree to tree, his hand resting on the hilt of his sword as he remained vigilant for any potential threats.

Lyra, the newest addition to the group, kept close to Leo's side, her expression a mix of excitement and apprehension.

Leo led the way with confidence, his gaze fixed on the path ahead as he plotted their course through the forest. Despite the gravity of their mission, there was an undeniable sense of camaraderie among the group, a shared determination to face whatever challenges lay ahead.

Suddenly, they stumbled upon a clearing where a massive creature lurked—a towering Treant. It resembled Mossweaver, but instead of the calm and wise demeanor of Leo's mentor, this was a true beast. It was also twice the size of Mossweaver.

Its branches were gnarled and twisted, and its eyes glowed with malevolence. The ground trembled beneath its massive roots as it roared, sensing the intruders in its territory.

"Holy crap," said Leo. "How come my mana awareness didn't pick that up?"

He used Identify.

Soulless Treant- (Level 97)

Strengths - Immense Strength: Despite its corrupted state, a soulless Treant retains its formidable physical power, capable of uprooting trees and crushing opponents with its massive limbs.

Necrotic Aura: The Treant exudes a dark energy that drains the life force of nearby living creatures, weakening them over time.

Weaknesses - Vulnerability to Fire: Being undead, the soulless Treant is highly susceptible to fire-based attacks, which can disrupt its necrotic essence and cause significant damage.

Limited Mobility: Despite its immense size and strength, the Treant's undead form may impair its agility and speed, making it vulnerable to agile opponents who can evade its attacks.

Lack of Intellect: As an undead creature, the soulless Treant has lost its capacity for reason and strategy, often acting on instinct alone. This makes it susceptible to manipulation and may lead to reckless behavior in combat.

Weakened Connection to Nature: The Treant's corruption has severed its connection to the natural world, rendering it vulnerable to spells or abilities that specifically target undead

creatures or disrupt dark magic.

A soulless Treant, also known as an undead Treant, is a terrifying entity that has been corrupted by dark magic or necromantic forces. It has lost its connection to the natural world and now exists as a twisted abomination of its former self.

Leo couldn't help but grin, despite the danger the party was in, because his Identify had gotten even more detailed than before.

"Happy days," he proclaimed. "Soulless, huh? That must be why my mana awareness didn't pick it up. No life force.

"Bradley, this thing don't like fire, so you're up. Jane, that new Holy Mana Bolt of yours, this fucker is vulnerable to anything that disrupts dark magic, so hammer it as much as you can.

"Buck, wait until the others have weakened it, then see if you can deal some damage. Lyra, go stealthy, and if you get a chance, stab the mother. Right team, let's do this."

The towering Treant stood before the party, its lifeless bark and gnarled branches stretching upwards to the canopy that obscured the sky. The feeble light that filtered through the dense foliage cast a haunting array of shadows on the ground beneath it. Its hollow eyes shone like fiery orbs, emanating an eerie and sinister aura that made the air around it feel thick and heavy.

Leo's commands sent a jolt of electricity through the team's veins, their hearts pounding with excitement as they prepared for the ultimate showdown. Bradley ignited a blazing inferno in his hands, ready to scorch the Treant into oblivion. Jane's eyes sparkled with a fierce determination as she unleashed a barrage of holy energy, determined to exploit the creature's every weakness. Buck flexed his bulging muscles, eager to prove his worth in the heat of battle, while Lyra disappeared into the shadows, her deadly daggers poised and ready for the perfect strike. The air crackled with adrenaline as the team braced themselves for the fight of their lives.

Leo stood poised to intervene if any of his party needed help, but he thought this was a good opportunity for them to up their Skills.

Bradley skillfully directed a steady stream of fire toward the Soulless creature, its intense heat engulfing the evil monster in a fiery inferno.

Meanwhile, Jane conjured up powerful Holy Mana Bolts which pierced through the creature's tough armor, leaving behind gaping wounds and causing it to writhe in agony. Together, Bradley and Jane fought bravely against the menacing monster, determined to defeat it.

But even though the two were doing a lot of damage, the Treant was massive, and being undead it could take a huge amount of injury. It lurched forward, stretching out its gnarled arms, reaching for Jane. But Leo stepped in, launching an immense mana bolt. Unlike Jane's bolts, this contained no Holy mana, but it was so powerful it smashed the monster back a few steps, enabling Jane to dodge away from its attack.

As the beast staggered backward, Buck saw his opportunity, and he leaped into the fray, lunging with his spear and hammering the wide blade into the creature's lower torso. Then he twisted the weapon savagely, pulled it out, and jumped back out of reach, taking advantage of the Treant's limited mobility.

Bradley launched a raft of fireballs, targeting the wounds that Jane had already opened up, and after a minute and six fireballs, the monster sank to its knees.

At that point, Lyra appeared out of Stealth mode, and showing remarkable dexterity, she scampered up the Treant's back and plunged her two daggers into each side of its neck. As Buck had done, she twisted the blades. Then she jumped off, disappearing into the shadows, once more in Stealth mode.

Buck stepped forward again, and this time he slammed his spear into the center of the Treant's forehead.

The monster gave out a shrill cry, and fell forward.

Leo finished it by launching a huge fireball that burned it to a pile of ashes.

"If you can't stand the heat," he quipped with a grin. "Well done, guys. Awesome job. You must have gotten a few Levels out of that, surely. I know I did, just by being a member of the party, although I did very little, it must be said."

"Level 13," said Bradley.

"Level 14," added Jane.

"Hey, I'm Level 11," interjected Buck. "And I got an upgraded class. I'm a Vanguard."

"And I'm now a Level 11 Shadowblade," announced Lyra.

"Good stuff, all," responded Leo. "Now. Let's loot this fucker and carry on. We got places to go and Pillocks to kill. Maybe."

CHAPTER 20

"Woah, that is a serious wall," said Leo as the party stared at the Pillocks village.

The wall was at least ten feet tall and was constructed from a combination of wood and stone. The craftsmanship was crude, but it was still an effective perimeter. The gate was made from large tree trunks, with leather hinges. They were closed and four guards stood outside them, armed with shields and spears.

The village appeared to house at least five hundred beings. The houses were simple wattle and daub with crudely thatched rooves, open windows without any form of glazing, and rickety doors.

"These guys might be vicious warriors," commented Leo. "But they don't seem to have progressed much with their building and crafting skills. A bit backward if you ask me."

"Umm … exactly why are we here?" asked Lyra, her voice barely above a whisper.

"Two reasons," answered Leo. "One, I wouldn't mind getting my mitts on that scroll. Sounds like that Lost City could give us a lot of sweet loot. And secondly, I really don't like these fuckers."

"Well obviously I don't either," concurred Lyra. "I hate them. But what can we do about that?"

"I reckon we'll just kill them all, and burn their shitty village to the ground. Might sound a bit harsh, but these dudes are vermin. I've only come across them twice, the first time they tried to kill me for no reason. And the next time they exterminated a peaceful village. Fuck them."

"It doesn't sound harsh," said Lyra. "But it does sound a little insane. There are over five hundred of them and five of us."

"Yeah, but one of us is me," replied Leo.

"You really think you're that powerful?" questioned Lyra, her voice expressing her skepticism.

"He is," interjected Buck. "I saw him take out hundreds of beasts when waves of them attacked our village."

Bradley nodded his agreement. "Dude is a fucking monster."

"What about women and children?" asked Jane. "Won't we be just as bad as them if we just kill everyone?"

Leo frowned but didn't answer. Instead, he looked more closely at the village and its inhabitants, as did the rest of the team.

After a couple of minutes of careful scrutiny, he spoke. "Weird. I don't see any women or children."

"Me either," agreed Bradley.

"That doesn't make any sense," interjected Jane.

"Yeah, because it's not like everything is so fucked up right now that anything actually makes any sense," said Leo. "Monsters, elves, random Pillock people who murder entire villages of innocents. Maybe the kids and families are underground. Maybe they live in a separate village from the warriors. Maybe … ah, fuck, who knows? And who cares? They are evil, they must be dealt with. With or without women and children."

"Okay," Jane conceded. "So, what's the plan?"

Leo licked his finger and held it up. "Firstly, I need to check which way the wind is blowing…"

***

"What is that?" asked Bradley.

"Poisonous gas," answered Leo. "Got it when I looted a drake. One of its attacks was a poisonous gas cloud. And trust me, this stuff is fucking deadly."

Leo pulled out two arrows from his quiver.

"The wind is blowing north," he explained. "So I'm gonna shoot these babies into the south side of the village. The wind should carry the resultant cloud over the whole area. We wait for it to disperse, then we bash down the gates, go in a mop up."

As Leo prepared the poisoned arrows, the air was thick with tension, each member of the party acutely aware of the imminent danger.

With practiced precision, Leo carefully tied the vials of gas to the arrows, his movements deliberate and focused. The weight of responsibility hung heavy in the air as the party braced themselves for the upcoming battle.

"Hold on," said Lyra. "Isn't the village out of bowshot?"

Leo grinned. "Not for me, I got mad skills."

With a steady hand, he nocked the first arrow and Imbued it with Wind, his gaze fixed on the south side of the village where the wind would carry the poisonous cloud across the entire area. The sound of his bowstring releasing echoed through the clearing, and the arrow soared through the air with deadly precision.

A microsecond later, the second one followed.

The arrows struck their mark, releasing the toxic gas into the atmosphere. A hazy cloud began to form, slowly drifting through the village like a silent harbinger of doom. The party watched with bated breath, their hearts pounding in anticipation of the chaos about to unfold.

As the poisonous gas enveloped the village, the distant sounds of coughing and retching reached their ears, signaling the Pillocks' unwitting exposure to the deadly toxin.

The Humanoids stumbled out of their homes, their faces twisted in agony as the toxic fumes invaded their lungs.

The thick and ominous gas cloud loomed

over the village, its ghastly green shade casting a haunting atmosphere over the area. The nauseating scent of decomposing matter mixed with the sharp and pungent aroma of the gas, overwhelmed the senses of anyone who came into even a short contact with it.

With each labored breath, scores of the Humanoids grew weaker, their movements becoming sluggish and uncoordinated. Many collapsed to the ground, writhing in agony as their bodies succumbed to the poison's deadly embrace.

Amidst the chaos, Leo and his companions watched from a safe distance, their hearts heavy with the weight of what they had unleashed. Despite the necessity of their actions, the sight of the suffering beings filled them with a profound sense of sorrow, but not of remorse.

They all remembered too well the sprawled, twisted corpses in the village the Pillocks had destroyed, men, women, and children. All were put to the sword, limbs dismembered, bodies violated and their property destroyed.

With a grim determination, Leo turned to his companions, his eyes blazing with resolve.

"The gas has dissipated. Let's move," he commanded, his voice cutting through the tense silence. "We've got scum to dispatch."

The team followed him towards the closed gates, running faster than any Olympic sprinter. As they ran, Leo equipped his axe. Then he Imbued it with both Wind and Lightning. Finally, he coated it with mana and extended the blades until they were over ten feet long.

Increasing his speed and pulling ahead of the others. First, he contemptuously dispatched the four guards, then he brought his axe down at a forty-five-degree angle and slashed through the gates like they were made of Paper Mache.

Lyra, who was close behind him, was awestruck at the casual power he had just shown. She knew the others had already told her, but seeing truly was believing.

Leo paused slightly as he got his bearings, and then he unleashed a barrage of mana bolts at any Pillocks still standing. "Be careful with your fire," he shouted to Bradley. "We don't want to burn this place down before we've found the scroll."

Leo rushed forward, wielding his axe in one hand while firing mana bolts with the other.

In all fairness, it was less a battle and more a massacre. The Pillocks that had survived the gas attack were weak, coughing and staggering around like zombies. Leo was culling rather than killing. Putting down a pack of vermin. And at the speed he could move, it didn't take long.

Mere minutes later, the village was quiet.

"Okay," he said as the rest of the team gathered around him. "I know that was unpleasant, but I truly believe it had to be done. If we hadn't taken these fuckers out, they would have attacked other innocent villages. Killed hundreds more innocent families. We did the right thing."

There was a general murmur of agreement from all.

"Now, I would guess that the scroll would be in the chief's house. So, let's look for the fanciest house and start there."

Finding the correct house was easy. While most of the houses were crude square bungalows, the chief's dwelling was two stories and had a wrap-around porch.

Jane found the scroll after a couple of minutes of searching. It was in the main bedroom, unrolled on the bed.

She handed it to Leo and he laced it on the kitchen table. They all leaned forward to read it.

"Congratulations, brave adventurers, for stumbling upon this ancient scroll. You must possess some semblance of wit and courage, or perhaps just sheer dumb luck. In any case, you have found yourself on the path to discovering the Lost City hidden within the depths of the forest.

But be warned, finding this city won't be as easy as following a map. Oh no, that would be far too simple. Instead, you'll have to rely on your wits and intellect to unravel the riddles and clues that lie within these ancient words.

Now, pay close attention, for here are your first clues:

Riddle 1:
I'm tall when I'm young and short when I'm old.
I'm hard when I'm cold and soft when I'm warm.

What am I?

Riddle 2:
I speak without a mouth and hear without ears.
I have no body, but I come alive with the wind.
What am I?

Now, follow these riddles to uncover the path to the Lost City. But remember, the journey may be perilous, and only the cleverest and bravest among you will succeed. Good luck, adventurers, and may the odds be ever in your favor."

"Seriously?" snapped Leo. "A couple of fucking schoolboy riddles and that's it?"

"They must give us a clue as to where the Lost City is," ventured Jane. "Let's work them out and see."

"Don't need to work anything out," said Leo. "It's fucking kindergarten stuff. The first one is – a candle. The second one – an echo."

"Man, boss," interjected Bradley. "You do a lot of riddles when you were a kid?"

Leo shrugged. "Yes… no …maybe. Whatever, how the hell does that help us?"

"Okay, let's think," said Lyra. "The first one, a candle. Maybe that suggests that we should look for something that resembles a candle in the forest, perhaps a structure or landmark that changes in appearance based on temperature or time."

"Nice one," agreed Bradley. "And the echo?"

"Could be we should listen for echoes or sounds carried by the wind, leading them to a specific location where the Lost City may be hidden. Additionally, the idea of echoes could symbolize the need to repeat certain actions or follow a repeating pattern to uncover the city's whereabouts."

"Brilliant," said Jane.

Leo sighed. "Look, I don't want to piss on anyone's parade, I admit that was some pretty serious lateral thinking there, Lyra. But it doesn't actually help us at all. I mean, what do we do, just wander around a vast forest listening for echoes and looking for candles? Hell, we don't even know what direction to start."

Lyra's expression fell. "True," she admitted. "What do you suggest?"

"I reckon we get out of this shit hole for a start," answered Leo. "And we burn the fucking place down on our way out. Then we hunt for some food, make camp, and rethink things."

The team nodded, they all were keen to leave the death and destruction that surrounded them.

Leo rolled up the scroll and put it into his Inventory.

As he did so, a message scrolled across his screen.

You have just stored a magical directional scroll. Would you like to add this magical scroll to your map?

Leo stopped. "What the…" he blurted out. "Yes, might as well."

A signal chimed in his head, and when he brought up his map, he could see a clear and visible path to the Lost City, complete with, obstacles and topography.

"Holy shit," breathed Leo. "Talk about a fucking Hail Mary. I knew this map couldn't just be a record of where I've been. Happy day," he turned to the team. "I know where we need to go," he said happily. "Now let's torch this place and get the hell outa Dodge."

CHAPTER 21

"Hey, where's the city at?" questioned Leo.

The team had followed his map and now, according to the directions, they were in the Lost City. Or at least very near it. But all they could see was a large entrance to a cave. Dark, damp, and forbidding, it gave off a palpable aura of menace.

"Maybe it's in the cave," suggested Jane.

Leo frowned, slightly embarrassed that he hadn't immediately assumed that. "Yeah, true," he concurred. "Let's go in and take a look."

The team's footsteps echoed through the damp chamber as they entered the cave, the dim light casting eerie shadows on the moss-covered walls. The air was thick with the musty scent of decay, and the distant sound of dripping water added to the ominous atmosphere.

A message chimed up on Leo's screen.

Congratulations.

You and your party have just entered the Lost City Dungeon. Be advised, that this is a level 50

dungeon, please ensure your party is capable of delving at this level.

Good luck – or not, frankly we don't give a shit.

"Hell, what's with the attitude," mumbled Leo. "Fucking System."

"What?" asked Jane.

"I just got a message, did you guys get one as well?"

They shook their heads.

"The System tells me that the Lost City is actually a dungeon. It also informed me that it's a level 50, so if you guys want to back out, this is your last chance."

"No way," said Buck. "We can do this."

"Okay," agreed Leo. "Let's go for it."

As the team entered the Lost City Dungeon, they were greeted by a sprawling underground metropolis that stretched out before them. Broken towers loomed overhead, their crumbling spires reaching towards the cavern ceiling. Cobbled streets wound through the city, illuminated by flickering lanterns powered by ancient magic.

The air was thick with the scent of damp earth and mildew, mingling with the musty odor of decay that permeated the abandoned streets. The sound of their footsteps echoed off the crumbling walls, creating an eerie symphony that reverberated through the deserted city.

"Wow, this place is huge!" exclaimed Jane, her

voice echoing softly against the stone walls. "It's like an entire city underground."

"It's definitely seen better days, talk about your fixer-upper," remarked Bradley, his eyes scanning the dilapidated buildings lining the streets. "But there's something... mesmerizing about it, don't you think?"

Buck nodded in agreement, his gaze fixed on the towering ruins looming in the distance. "I bet there's all kinds of sweet treasure hidden in these old buildings. We just have to find it."

Leo surveyed their surroundings, a sense of determination burning in his chest. "Let's stick together and explore carefully," he said, his voice steady despite the eerie surroundings. "Remember, this is a dungeon, and that means – we will be attacked at some stage. Most likely sooner, rather than later."

As they cautiously moved ahead, their footsteps echoed in the eerie silence of the underground cavern. Suddenly, the tranquility was shattered by a cacophony of battle cries and clashing of weapons. Leo's heart raced in his chest as he tightened his grip around his trusty axe, feeling the surge of adrenaline coursing through his veins.

In an instant, a horde of Goblins emerged from the shadows, their beady eyes glinting with ferocity. Without a moment's hesitation, the Goblins charged forward, their crude weapons raised high, ready to strike.

"Stay focused, everyone!" Leo shouted above the chaos, his voice tinged with determination. "Jane, stay back but keep us healed. Bradley, let's see some fire. Buck, take the front with me. Lyra, flank the little fuckers."

Leo charged forward, equipping his axe as he did. Buck ran behind him, unable to keep up with Leo's superhuman speed, but still giving it his all. Leo struck the wave of goblins like a battleship, swinging his Imbued axe in wide arcs, hacking some of the green-skinned creatures in half, dismembering some, and opening massive wounds on others.

Buck had finally caught up to Leo and stood resolute by his comrade's left shoulder. His spear, an extension of his fierce determination, danced through the throng of enemy soldiers with deadly precision. With each calculated thrust, he carved a path through the enemy ranks. Despite the overwhelming odds against him, Buck remained steadfast, his unwavering spirit burning bright in the face of adversity.

In the midst of the chaos, Lyra moved like a phantom in the shadows, her stealth allowing her to glide unnoticed through the tumultuous fray. With each strike, she attacked from behind, her daggers piercing through the enemy's weak points with lethal precision.

In the heart of the battle, Bradley stood like a fiery sentinel, his hands ablaze with the crackling energy of his fireballs. With a fierce determination etched on his face, he unleashed torrents of flames, each burst erupting in a dazzling display of light and heat.

The air filled with the acrid scent of burning flesh as the fireballs found their mark, engulfing groups of Goblins in searing heat. The crackling of flames mingled with the frantic shouts and cries of the enemy, their panicked movements betraying their fear of the inferno unleashed upon them.

As Bradley hurled fireball after fireball, his focus remained unwavering, his eyes fixed on the enemy before him. With each burst of flame, he felt a surge of exhilaration, a primal thrill coursing through his veins as he unleashed the full extent of his power upon the enemy horde.

"Feel the heat, you filthy snot-nosed pile of putrescent, ass-wiping Goblins," Bradley shouted, his voice ringing out above the roar of the flames. "No one messes with us and gets away with it."

While Bradley was busy thinking up more weird and wonderful insults, as well as throwing flame, he didn't notice one of the goblins crawl up to him. That is until the green-skinned vermin plunged a dagger into Bradley's thigh.

"Mother fucker," yelled the Flame Sovereign as he directed a gout of flame at his attacker. The flame struck the goblin in the face, burning off its flesh and killing it almost instantly.

Jane ran forward and cast a Healing spell on him. The deep wound in his thigh stopped bleeding, and the flesh knitted slowly back together.

"Thanks," he expressed his gratitude to Jane. "That hurt like hell."

"No worries. Now you get back to burning these SOB's."

Bradley blocked out the pain and continued his BBQ.

After another couple of minutes, Leo couldn't find any more goblins to dispatch. He paused and looked around. The cobbled streets were covered with corpses. Some burned to a crisp, others hacked to pieces. Green blood lay in puddles and the stench of viscera and fear filled the air.

"Tha...tha...tha...that's all, folks," he said.

Buck leaned on his spear, breathing heavily from the exertion. "Man, there must have been a couple of hundred of those things," he said.

Leo frowned. "Hey, you're bleeding."

Buck looked down at his torso and saw at least three wounds. One of them deep and wide. "Oh, crap. You're right."

Jane rushed over and did her thing. Soon Buck's bleeding stopped and he was mostly healed up.

Bradley walked over to one of the bodies and nudged it with his foot. "Loot."

Nothing happened.

"What gives?" he questioned. "Why no loot?"

"I've actually only been in one other dungeon," said Leo. "Albeit for quite a long time, and it was the same there. I couldn't get any loot from the bodies, but the dungeon did give me reward chests with loot in them."

"Like these?" asked Lyra, pointing at a row of five different-sized chests. They were all wood and bound in steel.

"How do we know who's is who's?" asked Bradley.

"Dunno," admitted Leo. "Let's take a closer look." He walked up to the row, picked up one of the smaller chests, and tried to open it. It remained firmly closed. "Strange," he said.

He turned and passed it to Bradley who was standing next to him. Still, no dice.

Jane was next, and as soon as she accepted the tiny chest it sprang open to reveal a row of five crystal vials filled with sparkling blue liquid. She used her limited Identify skill on it.

"It's a rare mana potion that replenishes magical energies," she said. "There's also this." She pulled out a small pouch and opened it up. It contained ten gold coins. She smiled. "Not exactly mind-blowing," she commented. "But still, not a bad little haul."

"We only fought the first level of mobs," said Leo. "As the difficulties increase, so will the rewards."

Leo bent down and picked up another chest, this one slightly larger, and handed it to Bradley, as he had done with the first one. Bradley tried to open it, then passed it to Lyra.

It opened, and inside was a pair of small gold

earrings.

Leo Identified them for her. "Enchanted earrings," he said. "They will slightly enhance your hearing and perception, and grant you improved awareness of your surroundings and the ability to detect hidden dangers."

"Not bad," said Lyra as she put them on, replacing the set of small silver hoops she already had on.

Buck stepped forward and touched the largest chest. It sprang open to reveal a pair of iron bracers enchanted to slightly enhance his strength and agility, allowing him to deliver more powerful strikes with his spear. "Nice," he said quietly as he donned them.

There were two chests left, and Leo picked up one of them. Sod's law, it was obviously for Bradley. He handed it over.

Bradley opened it, took out a scroll, and perused it.

"A scroll inscribed with a spell that will allow me to slightly, but permanently increase the power of my fire spells. Excellent."

Finally, Leo opened his reward. It was a small, dull copper-colored token, about the size of his palm. He Identified it.

"It's a stealth boot upgrade token," he announced. "I apply it to my boots and it makes me stealthier. Good one."

He immediately leaned down and pressed the token against his right boot, then he channeled some mana into it to activate the upgrade.

There was a shimmer of light and the token disappeared.

"Right, we're all done here," he said. "Let's proceed."

CHAPTER 22

"There's fuck all in any of these houses," moaned Buck after exiting yet another ruined dwelling. "I was hoping for some loot. Gold, maybe some armor. Anything. But it's like no one actually ever lived here. It's like an empty movie set."

"Yeah well, I reckon the only rewards we'll get will be provided by the dungeon.," said Leo. "Or the System, or whatever. Not entirely sure how this all works. But one thing I do know, seems that the System likes violence. If you don't kill things, then you don't get shit. Whatever the System is ... it's fucking psychotic."

As the team prepared to venture further into the dungeon's murky depths, they felt a palpable sense of anticipation. They knew that danger lurked around every corner, and the unknown made them extremely wary. The sound of their footsteps echoed through the dimly lit corridors, creating an ominous cadence that seemed to amplify the darkness. They braced themselves for the worst as they imagined the horrors that awaited them.

Suddenly, they heard a chorus of low and menacing growls echoing through the shadows, causing their hearts to race.

Out of the darkness emerged a pack of ferocious Wargs, their eyes gleaming with an insatiable hunger, and their snarls reverberating off the damp and rough-hewn walls, sending a chill down their spines.

Leo gripped his axe tightly, his heart racing with adrenaline as he looked out at the chaos before him. The weight of their mission felt like a heavy burden on his shoulders, but he knew that failure was not an option.

Greater Warg - (Level 47)

Strengths –

Speed and agility: Wargs are incredibly fast and agile, able to dart around their enemies with remarkable swiftness.

Powerful bite: Their jaws are lined with razor-sharp teeth, capable of inflicting severe injuries with a single bite.

Pack mentality: Wargs often hunt in packs, allowing them to coordinate their attacks and overwhelm their prey with sheer numbers.

Enhanced senses: They possess acute senses of sight, smell, and hearing, enabling them to track down their targets with precision.

Weaknesses –

Vulnerable to fire: Despite their fearsome

nature, Wargs are particularly susceptible to fire-based attacks, which can cause them to panic or retreat.

Limited endurance: While they excel in short bursts of speed and aggression, Wargs can tire quickly during prolonged engagements, allowing their opponents to gain the upper hand.

Pack dependency: Wargs rely heavily on their packmates for support and coordination in battle. When isolated or separated from their pack, they may become disoriented or less effective in combat.

The Warg is a formidable creature, resembling a large, wolf-like predator with sleek fur, sharp claws, and gleaming teeth. Its muscular build and keen senses make it a swift and deadly opponent in battle. With a menacing growl, it lunges at its prey with lightning speed, aiming to tear them apart with its powerful jaws.

"Stay close, everyone," Leo roared, his voice filled with urgency. "It's just a bunch of doggies, we've faced worse than this. You all know the drill, let's do this."

In the midst of a frenzied whirlwind of fur and fangs, the Wargs lunged forward with lightning speed, their sharp teeth bared and glistening in the dim light. Leo stood firm, his axe held tightly in his hand as he met the creatures head-on with a ferocious determination.

With each clash of blade against claw or

fang, the metallic clang echoed through the air, drowning out the sounds of their desperate struggle. Despite the searing pain that shot through his body as the creatures' teeth sank into his flesh, Leo pushed through, fueled by a surge of adrenaline and an unwavering resolve to protect his team at all costs.

The dungeon chamber flickered with an ominous glow as Bradley summoned his flames, the crackling fire illuminating the ferocious Wargs as they closed in. Sweat beaded on his brow as he focused his magic, the heat of his flames searing the air around him.

"Watch out for friendly fire," his voice rang out, a note of urgency tinging his words. "I haven't quite got my control perfect."

Despite his outward show of confidence, Bradley felt a twinge of fear gnawing at his gut as the Wargs surged forward, their gleaming teeth bared in savage snarls.

With a surge of adrenaline, Bradley unleashed a torrent of fire, the searing heat washing over the Wargs, driving them back. But as he focused on maintaining his flames, a sharp pain shot through his side, and he was thrown to the floor.

One of the Wargs had sprung forward and crashed into Bradley's back, hammering him to the floor, breaking at least two ribs, and driving the wind out of him.

"Get the hell off me, you fake-wolf piece of walking dogshit."

The Warg howled its anger and tried to bite Bradey in the face, but as it lunged forward, Bradley punched out a small, but intensely hot ball of fire. The fireball sizzled into the monster's right eye, burning through and directly into its brain. The Warg stiffened and then fell forward, pinning Bradley to the floor.

"Gah!" Bradley winced, his broken ribs protesting at the massive weight. "I'm stuck, guys. Get this smelly piece of crap off me!"

Buck ran over, and using his spear as a lever, he prized the Warg off Bradley, then without pause, he returned to the battle.

Jane knelt and laid her hands on her injured companion.

"Hmm – broken ribs, concussion, and a few minor cuts," she mumbled as she pushed her healing mana into him.

Bradley winced as his ribs popped back into place and knitted together. "Thanks, Jane," he said as he stood up, stretching his back and rolling his shoulders before conjuring up another fireball. "Time to get back on the grill," he continued as he launched the fireball at the closest Warg.

Amidst the chaos of battle, Lyra was a force to be reckoned with. Her lithe figure darted and weaved between the snarling Wargs, their menacing jaws snapping at her heels. But she was too quick for them, her movements shrouded in shadows that seemed to dance around her. With expert precision, she plunged her twin daggers into the beasts' soft spots, striking with the speed and agility of a seasoned warrior. It was a thrilling sight to behold, a testament to Lyra's unmatched skill and bravery in the face of danger.

The dimly lit dungeon echoed with the clash of steel and the growls of the Wargs, creating a cacophony of sound that filled the air. The scent of blood mingled with the musty odor of damp stone, adding to the intensity of the moment.

Despite her nimble agility, Lyra was not immune to the dangers of combat. A sharp pain shot through her side as one of the Wargs managed to land a solid blow with its razor-sharp claws, leaving behind a trail of blood. Gritting her teeth against the pain, she fought on, determination shining in her eyes as she refused to let her injuries slow her down.

Leo stormed over and swung his axe, chopping downward and cleaving the offending Warg in twain.

"Don't fucking bite my team members," he growled as he turned and plunged back into the swirling, howling pack, hacking and hewing.

Amidst the chaos of battle, Jane's heart clenched with worry as she caught sight of Lyra, her fellow teammate, wounded after being attacked by one of the snarling Wargs. Desperation flooded through her veins as she fought to reach her new friend's side, her healing instincts kicking into overdrive.

But the relentless onslaught of the Wargs

proved to be a formidable barrier, their savage attacks pushing Jane back with each attempt to reach Lyra. She could hear the sounds of their clash echoing around her, the ferocious growls and yelps of pain mingling with the clang of weapons and the desperate shouts of her companions.

Jane's anxiety was increasing with each passing moment, making her chest feel tight with fear for Lyra's safety. She gritted her teeth, feeling frustrated as she struggled to break through the Wargs' defenses. The air was filled with the scent of blood, which mixed with the earthy aroma of the dungeon, making the intensity of the moment even stronger.

"Jane, watch your back!" Leo's voice rang out above the din of battle, snapping her back to the present. "Focus on keeping yourself safe!"

Despite her concern for Lyra, Jane knew that she needed to heed Leo's words. But she was determined to reach the young Shadowblade. Taking a deep breath, she summoned her mana and unleashed a series of Holy mana bolts at the Wargs standing between her and Lyra.

Although not as effective as Bradley's fireballs, the Holy bolts still inflicted great pain upon the evil Wargs. Barking and whining, they scattered in an attempt to escape the burning blue bolts.

Jane took advantage of their momentary confusion, and she ran forward, jinking left and right until she reached Lyra.

A few seconds later, Lyra was all healed up,

and Jane turned and sprinted away from the fray, cognizant of Leo's warning to keep herself safe.

Meanwhile, Leo noticed that the pack of Wargs was starting to tire, and then he saw the Alpha Warg rallying them, snapping and snarling as he pushed them back into the battle.

"Yeah, I see you," muttered Leo to himself. He locked eyes with the Warg Alpha, its imposing figure towering over the frenzied pack. Determination surged through him as he gripped his axe tightly, ready to face the formidable foe before him.

With a roar of defiance, Leo charged forward, his muscles burning with exertion as he clashed with the Alpha in a battle of strength and skill. The sounds of their struggle filled the air, the clash of metal against fur echoing through the cavernous chamber.

Leo stood firm in the face of the Warg's ferocious attacks, refusing to yield an inch of ground to the snarling beast. With every movement, he displayed a fierce determination to protect his team.

Despite the searing pain that shot through his body when the Alpha's claws raked across his skin, he gritted his teeth and pushed through it. The adrenaline coursing through his veins fueled each swing of his axe as he fought back against the monstrous creature.

Leo's heart pounded in his chest as the battle roared on, his senses heightened and his focus honed in on the massive Warg before him. With each strike, he could feel the weight and power behind it, every movement fueled by a fierce determination to emerge victorious in this life-or-death struggle. He fought with every ounce of strength he possessed, refusing to back down in the face of his fearsome foe.

With a final, decisive strike, Leo delivered a crushing blow to the Alpha, its howls of pain reverberating through the chamber as it fell to the ground, defeated. With another swing, Leo decapitated the beast.

The pack, now leaderless, descended into disorder, their ranks breaking as they scattered in confusion.

Exhausted but triumphant, Leo stood amidst the chaos, his chest heaving as he surveyed the aftermath of the battle. Relief washed over him as he realized the danger had passed, his team safe for now.

None of them bothered to chase down the few members of the pack that had cut and run. Without an Alpha, they were no longer a threat.

"Where the reward chests at?" enquired Leo as he looked around.

Bradley pointed. Another row of five different-sized chests lay at the edges of the battle area.

After a bit of swopping, they each opened their respective chests.

Buck got a set of greaves that enhanced his speed and agility.

Bradley got a bracelet that increased his mana recovery time.

Jane got a spell scroll that allowed her to magically learn a Spell of Calm. An area effect spell that would envelop all within twenty feet of her with a feeling of peace and tranquility.

Lyra got a Cloak of Concealment. It wasn't quite a cloak of invisibility, but it did enhance her Stealth. Plus, it was nice and warm.

Leo received a spell book with ten spells in it. But when he uploaded it to his interface, he saw that the spells were all grayed out. "Fuck off," he cussed. "What's the use of that? It's like making a starving man watch someone cook a steak. I can see the spells, but I can't access them."

"Maybe it's timed or something," suggested Bradley. "You know, like each day, or week a spell is released."

Leo shrugged. "Maybe, whatever, nothing I can do about it. Let's move on a bit, then stop and eat something. Hey, I wonder what Warg steak tastes like? Bradley can start a fire and we can try some."

"Eewww," sneered Jane. "Gross."

"Why?" asked Leo.

"It's like eating a hyena," answered Jane.

"So? Maybe hyena tastes good. We don't know. Anyway, I'm gonna butcher one and cut some steaks. You don't have to eat any of it."

An hour later, they were all sitting around a campfire, eating chunks of skewered Warg meat.

"Okay, I was wrong," admitted Jane. "It's a bit

tough, but it's real tasty."

"You never know until you try," said Leo. "After his, I recommend we all meditate for a bit, get our HP and MP up. Then when we all feel fully rested, we proceed."

CHAPTER 23

As the team proceeded further down into the dungeon, their footsteps reverberated against the unforgiving stone floor, creating an eerie echo that seemed to follow them with each passing step. The air grew increasingly dense, and heavy with the unmistakable aroma of moist earth and a peculiar, musky scent that lingered in their nostrils. The darkness enveloped them, adding to the sense of foreboding that permeated the atmosphere.

A chilling skittering sound filled the air.

"What the hell is that?" questioned Leo. "Sounds like a million giant cockroaches. Fuck, don't let it be cockroaches, I hate those little fuckers."

"It's not cockroaches," noted Buck.

"Good," responded Leo.

Buck shook his head. "No, not good. It's worse."

Leo's pulse quickened as he squinted into the dimly lit chamber, his eyes narrowing at the sight of the approaching swarm of Giant Spiders. Their hairy legs moved with eerie precision, each step sending a shiver down his spine.

With a sense of urgency, Leo reached for his bow and quiver, the familiar weight of the weapon reassuring in his hands. Nocking an arrow, he focused his energy, channeling his magic to imbue it with crackling lightning.

"Here they come," Leo called out to his team, his voice steady despite the rising tension. "Stay sharp and watch your backs."

As the first spiders closed in, Leo drew back his bowstring. With a swift release, the arrow found its mark, striking true and exploding with a blinding flash of light that lit up the surrounding buildings and alleyways.

The creature convulsed as its insides became its outsides, guts spilling from the rent in its belly. It emitted a high-pitched screech that echoed through the chamber. Leo's heart raced as he unleashed arrow after arrow, each shot finding its target with deadly accuracy.

The dimly lit chamber flickered with dancing flames as Bradley unleashed torrents of fire, the crackling heat casting eerie shadows against the stone walls. With each burst of flame, the air filled with the scent of burning spider silk, mingling with the acrid aroma of charred spidey-flesh.

Bradley's face was illuminated by the fiery glow, his expression one of fierce concentration as he directed the flames, creating a fiery barrier that crackled and hissed with intense heat.

"Back, you creepy crawly, multi-eyed overgrown garden pests," he shouted, his voice echoing through the chamber as he pushed back against the advancing horde of spiders. "You look ridiculous with so many legs."

As the spiders recoiled from the searing heat, Bradley's flames served as a protective shield for his team, providing them with a brief respite from the relentless onslaught.

The cavernous chamber resounded with the deafening echoes of Buck's mighty strikes. His spear sliced through the air with unparalleled precision, unleashing shockwaves that reverberated through the room. With each thrust and parry, Buck's chiseled muscles bulged and flexed, embodying raw power and unbridled determination. His movements were graceful and calculated, his strikes like an unstoppable tempest.

He moved forward, and he was immediately greeted by a chorus of hisses and clicks from the spiders that scuttled back in fear as he advanced. With their multiple eyes fixed warily on him, Buck advanced without any hesitation, his spear gleaming in the faint light. The formidable presence of the warrior seemed to send shivers down the spines of the arachnids, who retreated further into the shadows, unwilling to face his might.

"Come on, you fuckers," Buck roared, his voice booming with confidence as he charged into the heart of the spider horde. "You want a piece of me? You got it."

Amidst the chaos, Lyra moved with the grace

of a phantom, her form weaving in and out of the shadows with effortless fluidity. With each step, her daggers flashed like silver lightning, striking with deadly precision as she danced around the spider horde.

The sounds of battle echoed through the chamber, but Lyra remained focused, her senses honed to a razor's edge as she anticipated the spiders' every move. With each attack, she dodged and weaved, her movements a blur of speed and agility as she darted between the creatures with unmatched finesse.

But as the battle raged on, a cry of alarm pierced the air as Buck found himself ensnared in a sticky web, his struggles only serving to entangle him further.

Lyra's heart skipped a beat as she watched her comrade's predicament, a surge of adrenaline coursing through her veins as she leaped to his aid.

"Hang on, Buck," she called out, her voice ringing with determination as she sprinted towards him. "I've got you."

With a swift movement, Lyra slashed at the web with her daggers, but even her ultra-sharp blades couldn't cut the gluey strands.

"Shit, shit, shit," shouted Lyra as a group of spiders approached them, venom dripping from their fangs. "I can't cut this stuff. It's like sticky steel cable."

Leo's heart sank as he saw Buck's predicament, knowing that drastic action was needed to free him.

He ran over, blasting spiders out of the way with both mana bolts and fireballs.

Drawing his Bowie knife, he too tried to cut through the webbing. But like Lyra, he had no luck.

"You gonna have to burn it off," yelled Buck. "And fast, I don't know what this stuff is made of, but I think it's got some sort of acid in it. I can feel it burning its way into me."

"I can't just burn it off," said Leo. "The amount of fire could kill you."

"Just fucking do it," shouted Buck.

With a heavy heart, Leo summoned his courage and unleashed a burst of flames, burning through the webbing and freeing Buck at last.

Buck screamed in agony as his flesh cooked and his hair caught alight, his body wracked with pain.

Leo pushed him to the ground and rolled him in the dirt to put the flames out.

Jane rushed to his side, her healing magic enveloping him in a warm glow as she worked to mend his wounds. Leo's chest tightened with guilt as he watched his friend suffer, but he knew it was a necessary sacrifice to keep them all alive.

Withdrawing a couple of Health potions from his Inventory, Leo poured them over Buck's burned face, and they immediately helped the healing process.

"Stay with him," he commanded Lyra. "Protect him. I'm gonna finish this."

Knowing he was in good hands, Leo stood up

and rejoined the battle.

Once Leo got going again, Bradley and he went full napalm on the rest of the arachnids, burning them to spider-crisps.

Then it was reward time.

The loot included poison antidotes for Jane, a spider silk robe for Bradley that was simply a self-repairing, self-cleaning really comfortable item of clothing, a reinforced helmet for Buck, and poison for Lyra's daggers.

Leo got one spell opened in his spell book. Wind manipulation - it allowed him to cast a spell that released a small but powerful whirlwind. He was well pleased.

CHAPTER 24

"I hate spiders," moaned Leo. "Just far too many legs. And eyes. And what is their obsession with the number eight? Eight legs, eight eyes. It's just fucking stupid."

"I thought you hated cockroaches, boss," interjected Bradley.

"Them too," admitted Leo." Actually, creepy crawlies, on the whole, give me the heebie-jeebies."

"Man, this Lost City is huge," said Buck. "I wonder how many more mobs we gonna have to fight. Also, what do you all reckon the Boss mob will be?"

Leo stared ahead, peering into the gloom. As he did so, a message flashed up on his screen.

Venomous Chimera - (Level 87) Boss.

Strengths –

Ferocious Strength: The lion's body gives the Chimera immense physical power, allowing it to overpower prey with ease.

Versatile Attacks: With three distinct heads,

the Chimera can unleash a variety of attacks, including slashing with its claws, biting with its lion head, and delivering venomous stings with its serpent tail.

Intimidating Presence: The Chimera's imposing size and fearsome appearance can instill terror in its enemies, making them more likely to flee or hesitate in combat.

Weaknesses –

Limited Agility: While powerful, the Chimera's size can also be a hindrance, making it less agile and maneuverable compared to smaller adversaries.

Limited Intelligence: The Chimera is often depicted as a creature of instinct rather than strategic thinking, leaving it susceptible to clever tactics and traps set by its foes.

The Venomous Chimera is a hybrid of several fierce animals. This species has the head and body of a lion, a second head, that of a goat emerging from its back, and a fully formed venomous serpent as a tail.

"The boss mob is a Venomous Chimera," said Leo.
"How the hell do you figure that?" asked Buck.
Leo pointed.
"Holy shit," murmured Bradley. "That is grotesque."

The towering beast loomed before them, a fearsome sight to behold. Standing at least ten feet tall at the shoulder, it boasted the muscular body and majestic head of a lion, its golden mane bristling with fury. But what truly unnerved them was the grotesque addition protruding from its midsection—a twisted, goat-like head with deranged, crimson eyes that seemed to pierce through their souls. Its long horns curved menacingly, adding to its eerie presence.

As if this wasn't enough to strike fear into their hearts, its tail, a sinewy serpent of at least ten feet in length, slithered with deadly intent. Its fanged maw snapped hungrily as its forked tongue darted in and out, hissing malevolently. The amalgamation of these creatures into one monstrous form sent shivers down their spines, and they knew they were facing a formidable adversary.

In the dimly lit dungeon, the monstrous chimera's deafening roars echoed off the walls, sending shivers down their spines. Leo clenched his jaw, his heart pounding in his chest as he stared down the beast before them. Gripping his axe tightly, he felt a surge of power coursing through him, fueled by his mana.

The creature snarled and twisted, preparing to defend itself against Leo's onslaught. But he remained undaunted, his eyes fixed intently on the task at hand. The chimera's growls echoed off the walls, filling the air with a menacing sound that only served to fuel Leo's determination.

As he closed the distance, Leo's movements became a blur of motion, his axe swinging with deadly precision as he unleashed a flurry of strikes upon the chimera. Each blow was fueled by his mana, the double blades extended by over six feet to deliver devastating damage with every swing.

As Leo's axe cleaved through the air, a crackling energy surrounded the weapon, illuminating the chamber with a pulsating glow. The room seemed to hum with anticipation as Leo's blade descended upon the chimera, the sound of metal meeting flesh echoing through the cavernous space like a thunderous drumbeat.

With each ferocious strike, sparks flew from the chimera's hide, the clash of metal against scales reverberating through the chamber with a deafening intensity. The air crackled with raw power as Leo's mana-infused blows found their mark, leaving deep gouges in the creature's flesh with each devastating hit.

Despite the chaos of battle, Leo remained focused, his movements fluid and precise as he unleashed a relentless barrage of attacks upon the chimera. Each swing of his axe was met with a resounding clang as it collided with the creature's armor-like skin, sending shockwaves rippling through the air with each impact.

But the Chimera was like no monster Leo had ever fought before. It may have been slightly cumbersome, and more than a little slow-witted, but it made up for those traits by being hyper-aggressive. On top of that, it must have had a massive amount of Constitution, as even the deepest of wounds that Leo had inflicted were already beginning to close up.

As Leo battled fiercely against the chimera, Bradley stood as closely as he could to the melee, his hands wreathed in flames as he summoned torrents of fire to engulf their monstrous foe. The chamber was illuminated with a flickering orange glow as the flames danced and crackled, casting long shadows against the walls.

The air was thick with the smell of burning fur and charred flesh, mingling with the metallic tang of blood and sweat as the team fought for their lives. Despite the intense heat, Bradley remained steadfast, his focus unwavering as he channeled his magic with precision, directing the inferno to sear through the chimera's tough hide.

With each blast of fire, the chimera roared in agony, its monstrous form writhing and thrashing in a desperate attempt to extinguish the flames. But Bradley pressed on, his determination unyielding as he continued to rain down fiery destruction upon their foe.

As the battle raged on, Buck charged towards the chimera with his spear in hand, moving with lightning-fast speed and unparalleled accuracy. His strikes were swift and precise, each one hitting the creature's weak points with deadly force, leaving it vulnerable to his attacks.

The sound of metal clashing against the chimera's scales reverberated throughout the chamber, blending with the creature's furious roars and the team's desperate shouts as they battled for survival. The air was tense and heavy, filled with the scent of sweat and blood as Buck pushed forward, his unwavering determination driving him forward despite the injuries he had sustained.

With each thrust of his spear, Buck felt the strain in his muscles and the sharp pain of his wounds, but he pushed through, fueled by the adrenaline of battle and the need to protect his comrades. He knew that Leo relied on him to cover his back, and Buck refused to let him down, but he was suffering. The goat head had managed to gore him in the side, and blood was pouring from the deep wound. The blood loss and the savage pain were draining his energy, and he wasn't sure how much longer he could keep up this level of attack.

Seeing that Buck had been severely wounded, Jane cast aside her fear and dashed toward him, her heart pounding with determination. Ignoring the looming threat of the chimera, she reached out and pulled Buck away from the fray, her hands gentle yet firm as she guided him to safety.

She laid her hands on Buck's wounded body, channeling her healing magic with focused intensity. The air around them shimmered with energy as Jane's healing powers surged forth, enveloping Buck in a warm glow of soothing light.

As she worked to mend his injuries, Jane felt a surge of empathy and concern wash over her. Buck's pain was palpable, his labored breathing and furrowed brow a testament to the severity of his wounds.

As the monstrous chimera thrashed and roared, Lyra moved with fluid grace, her movements a blur of speed and agility. With her daggers poised and ready, she danced around the beast with uncanny precision, her every strike calculated and swift.

The sound of her blades slicing through the air was like a whisper amidst the chaos, their poisoned tips gleaming in the dim light of the dungeon. With each precise strike, Lyra aimed for vulnerable spots on the chimera's hide, her movements guided by instinct and honed skill.

Despite the danger that surrounded her, Lyra remained focused and composed, her senses attuned to the ebb and flow of the battle. The scent of blood and sweat filled the air, mingling with the metallic tang of fear as the team fought for their lives against the formidable foe.

With each darting movement, Lyra sought to outmaneuver the chimera, her heart pounding with adrenaline as she danced on the edge of danger.

By now even Leo's prodigious strength and stamina were starting to bottom out, so he backed out of the close-quarter melee and equipped his bow instead.

Arrow after arrow struck the Chimera, exploding on contact and adding to its already extensive injuries.

Then disaster struck.

Lyra came out of stealth and plunged er daggers into the serpent's tail, just behind its head. But as she did so, she slipped on the blood that now covered the cobblestones, and as she fell, the serpent struck, sinking its venomous fangs deep into her left arm.

She immediately went into convulsions, falling to the floor and thrashing around as the powerful poison coursed through her veins.

"Leo," screamed Jane. "Help me."

"Buck, on me," commanded Leo. "Bradley, lay down covering fire. We gotta get this thing away from Lyra so Jane can treat her.

At the same time, Leo pulled a vial of healing potion from his Inventory and chucked it to Jane who caught it and nodded her thanks.

Leo stored his bow and equipped his Starforged spear. He tried to defeat the monster with axe and bow, now it was time for a good, solid stabbing.

Buck and he flanked the Chimera, Leo on its right, Buck on its left, while Bradley directed a torrent of fire at the creature's face. Moving backward as he did so, in an attempt to draw it away from Lyra.

At the same time, both Buck and Leo lunged forward, stabbing deeply into the Chimer's side.

The tactic worked as the enraged beast charged

at Bradley, roaring its anger, all caution thrown to the wind as it advanced.

Leo jumped high in the air, and brought his spear down on the top of the goat's head, between its horns. The blow was perfectly timed and the blade sunk deep, punching through its skull and penetrating deeply into its brain.

The head shivered once and then fell lifelessly down, obviously dead.

At the same time, Buck struck the serpent. Once, twice, and thrice, each blow slashing into the creature just behind its head where Lyra had already struck with her twin daggers.

The fourth blow finally severed the head from its body. Blood sprayed from the massive wound, and the serpent went limp.

The remaining head, the lion, went apoplectic as it sensed its other heads die. Waves of confusion swept over the beats, as it was used to receiving multiple areas of sensory input, three hundred and sixty-degree sight, the ability to attack from the front, side, and rear, and its ultimate weapon, the venomous serpent, were all gone. Now it was simply a large lion with some dead appendages.

Leo stored his spear and took out his axe.

"Time to die, you motherfucker."

He leaped forward, sweeping the axe down from on high and striking the lion laterally across its head, smashing its skull and dashing its brains out onto the cobbles below.

Leo immediately ran over to Jane and Lyra.

"How is she?" he asked.

Jane shrugged. "She's stopped fitting, but she's still unconscious."

Have you given her the health potion?"

Jane shook her head. "She's completely out. I can't get her to swallow it."

"Pass it here," said Leo as he knelt next to the prone body. Then he opened her mouth and trickled the potion in, gently massaging her throat to induce her to swallow. It worked. A painstakingly slow process, but an effective one.

It took over two minutes to get the potion down her, and five minutes after that, with Jane still spamming health cures on her, Lyra's eyes flickered open.

"I'm alive."

"You sure are," said Leo with a smile. "How do you feel?"

"Like shit," replied Lyra. "Hey, boss," she continued.

"Yep."

"Can I be a disciple as well?"

"Oh, for fuck's sake," grumbled Leo.

And then there were four.

Buck's rewards were a shield and an upgrade token for his spear. When he used the token, his spear changed from low-grade wood and iron to something resembling Leo's Starforged spear.

Jane received a spell scroll that would now allow her to heal at a distance. At the moment it was from up to ten feet, but as the spell leveled up the distance would increase.

Bradley received a spell scroll. Emberstorm, the ability to rain down a relentless barrage of fiery embers from the sky, engulfing enemies in a fiery inferno and leaving them charred and smoldering.

Lyra got a bow and arrow plus a Skill scroll so she got the skill of archery at a starting level. She was pleased that she would now have a ranged attack.

And finally, Leo had two more spells opened up, as well as an upgrade to his Tornado spell. The two new spells were, Heal over time, a less powerful version of Jane's ability, but still very useful. And Pyroclasm. The ability to channel the power of a volcanic eruption, sending molten lava cascading down upon enemies, dealing massive damage over time.

"Yeah," Leo punched the air. "Who's a mega-spell-making motherfucker? Me," he continued. "The answer is me."

The rest of the team laughed out loud.

Leo checked out his Stats to see what he had gained.

He was now Level 65 and he threw his points into Wisdom, figuring with more access to spells, he would need to up his mana.

"Nice one, guys," he said. "Let's get the fuck outa here."

Character Name: Leo Armstrong (Human)

Class: *Stormcaller Archmage-Hunter*

Titles: *Friend of the Elves*
Warrior Lord
Cyclops Slayer

Level: 65

Experience Points (XP): 8200000/9000000

Stats:
- **Strength (STR):** 559
- **Dexterity (DEX):** 504
- **Constitution (CON):** 854
- **Intelligence (INT):** 514
- **Wisdom (WIS):** 594
- **Charisma (CHA):** 453

Stat points available - 0

Note - 5 Stat points are made available during each Level gained.

Skills:
- **Axe Throwing (Level 12):** subject is skilled in throwing axes accurately, dealing damage from a distance.

- **Survival (Level 15):** subject can navigate through wilderness, track animals, and find resources efficiently.
- **Archery (Level 27):** subject is proficient with a bow, allowing him to shoot arrows with power and accuracy.
- **Camping (Level 6):** subject excels at setting up camps, building fires, and surviving in outdoor environments.
- **Cooking (Level 7):** The subject can prepare simple and nutritious meals using outdoor ingredients.
- **Axe Wielding (Level 33):** subject can wield an axe with a good degree of proficiency.
- **Lighting Infusion (Level 20):** subject can infuse his arrows with the power of a Thunderbolt.

Wind Infusion (Level 22): subject can infuse his arrows with the power of the Wind, this allows the arrow to travel further, faster and with more accuracy.

Spear Wielding (Level 20): subject is now proficient in spear combat.

Mana Manipulation & Core Control (Level 37): subject can now actively affect external mana.

Dagger Wielding (Level 4): subject can now use his dagger to deal death.

Whirlwind Spell (Level 1): subject can unleash a small whirlwind.

Pyroclasm (Level 1): subject can channel the power of a volcanic eruption, sending molten lava cascading down upon enemies, dealing massive damage over time.

Heal Over Time (Level 1): a weak healing spell that allows the subject to do a moderate amount of healing.

Inventory:

- **Weapons:**
  - Throwing Axes (x2)
  - Battle Axe
  - Bowie Knife
  - Bow of Storms (Soulbound)
  - Quiver of Antiquity (Soulbound)
  - Starforged Spear (Soulbound)

- **Armor:**
  - Leather tunic with metal scales (Self-repairing, self-cleaning)
  - Vambrace (x2) (Self-repairing, self-cleaning)
  - Reinforced Leather Boots (Self-repairing, self-cleaning) Have been upgraded to provide extra Stealth
  - Stout leather trousers with metal scales (Self-repairing, self-cleaning)

- **Consumables:**
- Healing Potion (2)
- Rations (3 days)

- **Tools:**
- Flint and Steel
- Compass
- Climbing Gear

- **Miscellaneous:**
- Map of the RPG Earth
- 720 gold coins
- Verdant Moonlight Amulet (Rare)
- 5 x Iron Wolf pelts
- 2 x Drake meat
- 2 x Warg haunches
- 5 x Cured drake hide
- 2 x Vials poisonous gas
- 2 x Drake claws
- 1 x Spell book

Quest Log:

- **Main Quest - The RPG Awakening:**
- Investigate the transformed world.
- Level up.

- Do not die.
- Train your four disciples to become better warriors.
- Remove the Corrupted Orc scourge from the forest, destroy their village, and put an end to the Darkness.

CHAPTER 25

As Leo and his companions continued to trek further into the forest, the atmosphere around them gradually underwent a subtle transformation. They could sense a faint murmur of enchantment that seemed to be emanating from the very heart of the woods, seeping through every crevice of the surrounding trees and caressing their skin with its gentle touch.

The dense foliage overhead filtered the sun's rays into a mesmerizing tapestry of gilded light, casting an otherworldly radiance upon the forest floor, which seemed to be alive with a pulsating energy.

As they ventured deeper, the air became thick with the sweet scent of wildflowers and earthy moss, while the melodic chirping of birds and the soft rustle of leaves added to the enchanting symphony of nature. Soon, they stumbled upon a clearing bathed in dappled sunlight, where a verdant glade stretched out before them like a lush, emerald carpet.

In the heart of this grove, Leo and his

companions discovered a gathering of wondrous creatures unlike any they had ever encountered. Lively sprites flitted about, their iridescent wings shimmering in the golden light, while graceful deer grazed peacefully nearby. Tiny woodland creatures scurried between the roots of ancient trees, their eyes sparkling with curiosity as they observed the newcomers with cautious interest.

"Wow, look at this place," Jane exclaimed in awe, her voice barely above a whisper as she took in the breathtaking sight before them.

"Yeah, it's like some sort of enchanted fucking forest," Bradley remarked, his eyes wide with wonder.

Leo couldn't help but feel a sense of reverence wash over him as he beheld the serene beauty of the enchanted grove. "We must tread lightly here," he cautioned his companions, his tone hushed with respect. "These creatures are guardians of the forest, and we're just guests in their realm."

With a shared nod of understanding, the team proceeded cautiously, their senses heightened as they approached the inhabitants of the grove. They were met with a chorus of melodic chirps and gentle rustles, as the woodland creatures regarded them with curious eyes, their expressions a mixture of inquisitiveness and wariness.

As Leo and his companions made their way into the grove, their senses were awash with a symphony of joyful sounds. Chirping birds sang in unison with the rustling leaves of the trees, and the soft rustle of animals scampering through the underbrush. The air was alive with tiny sprites, flitting through the air like living sparks of light, and woodland creatures peeking out from behind bushes and tree trunks.

The inhabitants of the grove, from the mischievous pixies to the wise old owls, welcomed the newcomers with open arms, their eyes shining with curiosity and warmth. The scenery was so enchanting that it felt like a scene from a fairy tale.

"Welcome, travelers," chirped a sprite, its wings shimmering with iridescent colors.

Then it bowed, while still in the air. "It is a great honor to greet one who is both Tree-bound and a Friend of the Elves."

Leo used Identify and was surprised to receive no information on the creature's Level, or its strengths or weaknesses.

Forest Sprite – (Level ?)

A tiny, ethereal creature standing no taller than a human hand. With a delicate and androgynous form, the forest sprite embodies the timeless magic of the woodland realm.

Despite its diminutive size, the forest sprite possesses a powerful aura of magic, its very presence imbued with the ancient energies of the woodland realm. It is a creature of boundless curiosity and mischief, flitting from flower to flower with the agility of a hummingbird and

spreading joy and wonder wherever it goes.

Leo assumed the lack of information was due to the creature's high magical affinity and he studied the magical creature with great interest.

Its slender body was draped in garments woven from the finest threads of spider silk, adorned with petals and leaves that seemed to shimmer with an otherworldly light.

At the center of its back were two iridescent wings, translucent membranes that caught the sunlight and refracted it into a dazzling array of colors. With each gentle flutter, the delicate wings propelled the sprite through the air with graceful ease, allowing it to navigate the dense foliage of the forest canopy with effortless agility.

The sprite's features were delicate and refined, with high cheekbones, a pert nose, and eyes that sparkled like dewdrops in the morning sunlight. Its skin, the color of polished marble, seemed to glow with an inner radiance, suffusing the surrounding air with a soft, ethereal light.

All around them, more sprites danced among the sun-dappled leaves, their laughter ringing out like the chiming of tiny bells, filling the air with a sense of enchantment and delight. They were guardians of the forest, custodians of its secrets, and symbols of the enduring magic that lay within its ancient depths.

Leo was enchanted and in awe of the feelings of joy that the sprites exuded.

He let his mana awareness expand, taking in all of the magical life around him. And he was surprised to come across a familiar aura, similar to Mossweaver.

"You have a drus here," he said to the sprite.

"Yes," confirmed the little creature. "We have many. Their leader is called Everbark. He is one of our elders. He actually foretold of your coming."

"How did he know?" asked Leo.

"He is a Visionary. He told us that a great Warrior Lord who is Tree-bound and a Friend of the Elves would come to our aid in our battle against the Darkness. Although he did not mention any of your friends."

"Disciples, actually," interjected Bradley.

"Friends as well," added Jane.

"Oh, I did not know you were a Holy Man," said the sprite.

"I'm not," denied Leo. "It's just these guys … they …whatever. Can I meet this Everbark?"

"Of course," answered the sprite. "He is in the sacred grove. Follow me."

"What is your name?" Jane asked the sprite.

"I am, Willow, lead sprite and keeper of the knowledge."

The team followed Willow deeper into the forest for a couple of hundred yards. And there they came across a circle of the largest trees Leo had seen to date. Seven massive Oaks, perhaps five hundred feet high, and wider than an apartment block. In a world without magic, such a huge living structure would have been an impossibility. But in the new System-enhanced world, it seemed that anything was possible.

Leo could sense the presence of the ents, but he still couldn't see them. What he did see was a bevy of what were obviously dryads, all gathered in the center of the grove.

They were small. Perhaps three feet tall. They were all beautiful young woman with long flowing, multihued hair, their bodies clothed in woven leaves and flowers. Their skin, and you could see a lot of it, what with leaves and flowers not being the most concealing of garments, had a faint greenish hue, blending seamlessly with the natural surroundings.

Their emerald green eyes were bright and radiant, reflecting the wisdom of the forest. But they also radiated a feeling of mischief and humor. And Leo could feel their gazes upon him as they studied him with unabashed interest, giggling and smiling.

Leo waved at them and smiled back.

"Perv," grinned Jane.

"Hey, they're pretty. And they look real friendly," replied Leo.

"And you know what they say," interjected Bradley. "Whoever they might be."

"No," said Jane. "What do they say?"

"You know," said Bardley, not answering but looking a little embarrassed.

"He's talking about the stories about Drayads

capturing human males and forcing them to have sex with them so they can procreate," said Lyra.

"Seriously?" gasped Jane. "Why?"

"Because there's only female Dryads," said Leo "No men. But that wasn't why I waved. I was just being friendly."

"Sure," smirked Bradley.

Before Leo could continue arguing a powerful presence entered his mana awareness field. He whipped his head around to see what it was, and he came face to face with a massive, towering version of Mossweaver.

Without thinking, Leo took a knee.

Seeing their leader's reaction, the rest of the team followed, surprised at his show of obsequence.

"Please, stand, Lord Warrior," said the ent, its voice rumbling like a summer storm. "My name is Everbark, and I greet you with joy and respect."

"And I greet you, great Everbark. With joy and reverence," replied Leo, the strangely archaic sounding greeting coming naturally to him as if he had always known it. "Willow mentioned that you were expecting me."

Everbark chuckled. "Perhaps the term expecting was a trifle strong. Let us rather say, I felt an approaching power.

"She also mentioned that you needed some help."

"Ah, yes," concurred Everbark. "That is true. Let me get straight to the point. We are having a problem with a tribe of Corrupted Orcs."

"I know orcs," said Leo. "But what the hell is a Corrupted one?"

"They are orcs that have been twisted or mutated by dark magic, curses, or demonic influence, becoming more monstrous and less humanoid in appearance. In this case, they have been transformed by a Dark Mage who for some reason has a vendetta against us and our people. They have been tasked with destroying our sacred grove as well as the surrounding forest. The only reason we are still here is due to the fact that we take care of the forest, and it conspires against the orcs in order to protect us. But it is only a matter of time before they find us. Then all will be lost."

"Not necessarily," said Leo. "I mean, the sprites have powerful magic, as do you. Not sure about Dryads, but you could take the orcs out, I'm pretty sure."

Everbark shook his head. "Corrupted Orcs are impervious to almost all magically based attacks."

"Holy crap, seriously? So if I chuck a fireball at them, what happens?"

"The fire will simply sputter out as it reached them. As will mana bolts, although Holy mana bolts may have some limited success. But for any attack to be truly successful, it has to be physical. An axe, a sword, an arrow. And orcs are fearsome warriors, the corrupted ones even more so. We are a peaceful people, we know nothing of battle. Even our spells are those of healing and growth.

Nothing violent."

"Tell me more about these Corrupted Orcs. The more info I have, the better."

"Physically, they are twisted and contorted, their features warped into grotesque visages of rage and agony. Their skin, once rugged and weathered, now bears grotesque protrusions and pulsating boils, oozing with vile ichor.

"Their eyes glow with an eerie crimson light, devoid of any semblance of humanity. Fangs protrude from their maws, elongated and razor-sharp, and dripping with venomous saliva.

"Driven by an insatiable hunger for destruction, corrupted orcs rampage across the land, leaving devastation in their wake. They heed no call but that of their dark master, enslaved by the very powers that have twisted their forms."

Everbark sighed. "These abominable creatures are an affront to nature itself."

"Doesn't sound good," said Leo. "How many?"

"Perhaps fifty," answered Everbark. "Perhaps less, but not more."

"I'll need to do a bit of recon work," said Leo. "Does anyone know exactly where this tribe lives?"

"Yes, Willow can show you," replied Everbark. "They took over a small village a few hours walk from here, killing all of the peaceful inhabitants when they did."

"Serious assholes," said Leo in disgust. "Look, Bradley, if you want out of this one that's fine," said Leo.

"Why?"

"Wel, you're not a melee fighter, and your magic won't work."

"My fire can still burn other shit, like fences, walls, buildings. I'm in, boss."

"Nice one," said Leo. "Right, Willow, lead on."

As Leo and his companions followed Willow, the forest seemed to come alive around them, vibrant and teeming with life. Sunlight filtered through the canopy above, dappling the forest floor with patches of golden light. The air was filled with the sweet fragrance of wildflowers and the earthy scent of moss and damp soil.

Birds chirped melodiously overhead, their songs blending harmoniously with the gentle rustle of leaves in the breeze. Oversized squirrels scampered along the branches, their bushy tails twitching with excitement as they darted from tree to tree.

As they made their way further into the dense and sprawling forest, a subtle yet undeniable shift in the landscape began to take hold. The once luxuriant foliage that surrounded them grew increasingly sparse and sickly, with the vibrant shades of green that once dazzled the eye fading into muted and lifeless hues of gray and brown.

The air itself grew heavy and oppressive, thick with a palpable sense of foreboding that seemed to cling to every passing breath. Even the sweet and heady scent of wildflowers that had perfumed the air just hours before was replaced by a foul and cloying stench of decay, as though some unseen force was slowly rotting away the very heart of the forest itself.

Leo and his companions exchanged uneasy glances as they pressed on, Willow leading the way with unwavering determination. The sounds of the forest grew eerily quiet, replaced by a haunting silence.

As they ventured deeper into the corrupted forest, the atmosphere grew increasingly oppressive. The once majestic trees now stood twisted and contorted, their gnarled branches reaching out like bony fingers grasping at the darkening sky. The air was heavy with a sickly-sweet stench, like rotting vegetation mingled with the metallic tang of old blood.

Leo and his companions navigated the treacherous terrain with caution, their footsteps muffled by the dense undergrowth that seemed to writhe and coil beneath their feet. The ground was uneven and treacherous, littered with jagged rocks and tangled roots that threatened to trip them with every step.

Despite the growing sense of unease that gnawed at their nerves, Leo and his companions pressed on, their determination unwavering in the face of the encroaching darkness. They knew that the corrupted orc tribe posed a grave threat to the forest and its inhabitants, and they were resolved to confront this evil head-on.

With each passing moment, the air seemed to

thicken with malevolence, and Leo could feel the weight of the forest's corruption pressing down upon him like a suffocating blanket. But he refused to be deterred, his heart filled with righteous fury as he prepared to face whatever horrors awaited them in the heart of the darkness.

"Damn, this place sucks," said Leo, his voice just a whisper.

"Yeah," agreed Bradley. "Smells like ass."

"We are close," said Willow. "Be careful, they sometimes have patrols out."

As Leo and his companions approached the village, they were greeted by a scene of utter desolation. The once-thriving community lay in ruins, its cottages had been ruined through neglect and were now mere broken hovels, barely standing amidst the filth and decay that surrounded them. The stench of feces and rotting food hung heavy in the air, assaulting their senses with its putrid odor.

The corrupted orcs, their bodies twisted and deformed by dark magic, lounged lazily around flickering fires, their faces contorted into grotesque masks of rage and despair. Boils and sores marred their ravaged skin, oozing pus and ichor onto the ground below. Long, jagged fangs protruded from their snarling mouths, dripping with venom.

Amidst the chaos of the village, some of the corrupted orcs lay sprawled on the ground, victims of the foul concoctions they brewed from whatever scraps they could scavenge. Their faces contorted in grotesque expressions, they seemed lost in a drunken stupor, oblivious to the world around them.

"Looks like Everbark was right," whispered Leo. "Seems to be around forty that I can see, so depending on how many are on patrol, and how many might be inside the houses, there's most likely fifty or so."

"That's a lot," said Buck. "Ten to one ain't exactly great odds."

"You got any more of that poison gas?" asked Bradley.

Leo shook his head. "No, but check them out. Loads of them are drunk or stoned or something. Whatever, I don't reckon those have got much fight in them. I wonder, Everbark says that magic won't affect them, but what about the buildings and stuff next to them?"

Jane shrugged. "No idea. Willow, what do you think?"

"I don't think they have any type of blanketing aura," ventured the sprite. "If I had to guess, I would say that your magic will work on the buildings, but not directly on them."

"I suppose the only way to find out is to try," said Leo.

Leo and his team advanced towards the village with utmost caution, their movements precise, calculated, and silent. Every step they took was deliberate, every breath measured, as they sought to evade the notice of the corrupted orcs that lurked in the area. The atmosphere was charged with an almost palpable tension, as if the very air around them was alive with the sense of danger that permeated the surroundings. The sound of their heartbeats thudded in their chests, a constant reminder of the perilous situation they found themselves in.

"Stay low and keep quiet," Leo whispered to his companions, his voice barely more than a breath. "As soon as we're in range, Bradley, I want you to hit the buildings hard. I'm gonna Imbue some arrows and shoot the fires they're all sitting around. Jane, use those Holy mana bolts. Buck, Lyra, wait for my command to rush them."

The team nodded.

As Leo and his team approached the edge of the village, their hearts pounded with anticipation. Leo gave the signal and the attack began. With lightning-fast reflexes, he drew his bow and fired an arrow that glimmered with explosive magic.

The arrow soared through the air and struck the nearest campfire, causing a massive explosion that sent flames and debris flying in all directions. The air was filled with the deafening roar of the explosion as fiery pieces of shrapnel peppered the surrounding orcs.

Bradley followed suit, conjuring torrents of fire that engulfed the surrounding buildings, their wooden frames crackling and groaning as they succumbed to the inferno. The acrid smell of burning wood filled the air, mingling with the stench of smoke and charred flesh.

Jane focused her mana, summoning bolts of holy energy that arced through the air and struck the corrupted orcs with searing intensity. The orcs howled in pain as the magic seared their flesh, but some of them were getting their act together as they realized they were under attack.

Spears, shields and swords were brought to hand, and they began to form up, yelling and shouting.

"Come on," commanded Leo as he equipped his axe and ran forward. "Let's ice these fuckers."

CHAPTER 26

Leo, Buck, and Lyra charged into the heart of the corrupted orc village, their hearts pounding with adrenaline as they faced the looming threat before them. The air crackled with tension as they plunged into the fray, their weapons at the ready and their minds focused on the task at hand.

As Leo charged into the heart of the fray, his battle cry echoed through the village, a defiant roar against the encroaching darkness. Gripping his axe tightly, he swung with relentless force, the blade cutting through the corrupted orcs with a meaty thwack. The firelight danced upon the steel, casting an ominous glint that mirrored the determination in Leo's eyes.

With each swing of his weapon, Leo felt the weight of responsibility upon his shoulders, a solemn promise to protect his companions and rid the land of the malevolent force that lurked within the village. His muscles burned with exertion, but he pushed through the pain, his resolve unyielding in the face of adversity. He concentrated purely on attack, trusting in Buck's skills to protect him from being flanked.

The corrupted orcs lunged at him with gnashing teeth and clawed hands, but Leo met their ferocity with his own, meeting every blow with a swift counterattack. Each strike fueled his determination, a burning desire to see justice served and the darkness banished from their midst.

Beside Leo, Buck stood like an unyielding bulwark against the tide of corruption, his spear and shield a testament to his unwavering resolve. With each swing and thrust, he moved with the grace of a seasoned warrior, his movements fluid and precise as he deflected the onslaught of attacks from their adversaries.

As the corrupted orcs surged forward, Buck met their advance head-on, his shield raised in a steadfast defense against their onslaught. With a swift flick of his wrist, he parried their blows with practiced ease, the sound of metal clashing against metal ringing out in the chaos of battle.

Despite the ferocity of their enemies, Buck remained unshaken, his focus honed on protecting Leo and the rest of the team at all costs. With each strike, he fought not only for their survival but for the very soul of the land.

Through the din of battle, Leo could hear Buck's voice, a reassuring presence amidst the chaos. "Keep pushing, boss. We've got this," he called out, his words a beacon of strength in the darkness.

In the midst of the chaotic fray, Lyra moved with the grace and precision of a phantom, her form a blur as she weaved effortlessly between the shadows. With each step, she left behind only a fleeting whisper, her movements so silent that even the keenest ears would struggle to detect her presence.

As the corrupted orcs lunged forward with snarling ferocity, Lyra met their aggression with an agile grace that seemed almost supernatural. Her daggers flashed in the firelight, their keen edges slicing through the air with deadly precision.

With each strike, Lyra targeted her foes with ruthless efficiency, aiming for vulnerable spots and exploiting weaknesses with calculated precision. Her attacks were swift and decisive, leaving no room for hesitation as she danced around her enemies with a fluid grace that belied her deadly intent.

Through the haze of battle, Leo caught glimpses of Lyra's form darting through the shadows, her movements a mesmerizing display of agility and finesse. Despite the chaos unfolding around them, he couldn't help but marvel at her skill.

As the battle raged on, Bradley and Jane remained on the outskirts of the fray as they provided support from a distance.

Bradley summoned torrents of fire that rained down upon the village, engulfing the buildings in flame. And even though his magical fire could not directly harm the corrupted orcs, the flames from the burning houses sure did.

The flames danced and crackled with ferocious intensity, engulfing the village in a fiery maelstrom that illuminated the night sky with an eerie glow. The air was thick with the acrid scent of smoke and burning flesh, a stark reminder of the devastation wrought by Bradley's infernal magic.

Jane's Holy mana bolts continued to sear their way into the orcs, but then she moved closer in order to cast her ranged healing on Buck and Leo who were both taking a lot of damage.

Leo spun and swung, his axe cleaving through any orc stupid enough to get close to him. And they were pretty much all stupid. Neither Buck nor he showed any mercy. Buck skewered any of the drunken orcs that lay on the ground, and Leo dispatched the rest, regardless of whether they threw their hands up in surrender or not.

Finally, the last one fell.

Buck did a quick check that they were all actually dead, dispatching those who were playing possum, or merely wounded. When the gristly task was done, he joined the rest of the team.

"Victorious," he said with a grin.

There was a round of high-fives and a few shouts of jubilation at a job well done, and at being not dead.

Until Leo interrupted them. "Uh, guys," he said. "I just checked out my Stat sheet, and we got a problem."

"What?" asked Jane.

"I was given a quest by the System when we set off for here. Remove the Corrupted Orc scourge from the forest, destroy their village, and put an end to the Darkness."

"Yeah, well I think we pretty much did that," interjected Bradley. "Orcs are 0 for 1."

"Then why is the quest notice still up?" questioned Leo.

"Shit," said Buck. "Because it isn't complete."

"The Dark Mage," said Jane. "Did anyone see someone who might have been the Dark Mage? Because if he's still around, he can corrupt more orcs."

"Yeah," agreed Leo. "Until we exterminate that fucker, we haven't sorted the problem."

"But how the hell do we find him?" questioned Bradley with a snort of frustration.

Before anyone could answer, a massive bolt of dark mana blasted out of the forest, heading straight for the team.

Buck threw his shield up and stepped into the path of the dark bolt. His shield deflected the magic missile, but the impact smashed him off his feet and threw him over twenty yards away.

"Shit," yelled Leo. "I think he just found us."

A male orc came floating out of the woods, buoyed up by magic.

Leo Identified him.

Orcish Dark Mage – (Level 92)

Strengths –

Mastery of Dark Magic: Orc dark mages wield powerful spells that can unleash devastating effects on their enemies.

Commanding Presence: Their imposing stature and intimidating aura instill fear in their foes, often causing them to falter in battle.

Weaknesses –

Vulnerability to Holy Magic: Dark magic is inherently opposed to holy magic, making orc dark mages susceptible to attacks imbued with divine power.

Physical Weakness: Despite their formidable magical abilities, orc dark mages are physically weaker than their warrior counterparts, making them easier targets in close combat.

Arrogance: Some orc dark mages are overconfident in their abilities, leading them to underestimate their opponents or become reckless in battle, which can be exploited by savvy adversaries.

In battle, the orc dark mage is a formidable adversary, their spells weaving a deadly tapestry of destruction that leaves their foes trembling in fear. With a guttural incantation, they unleash torrents of dark energy that sear the air with their malevolent power, laying waste to all who

dare oppose them.

Despite their fearsome appearance and mastery of dark magic, orc dark mages are not invincible. Their reliance on the corrupting influence of the dark arts leaves them vulnerable to the purifying light of holy magic, and their physical prowess pales in comparison to their warrior brethren. Yet, their cunning intellect and mastery of the arcane make them a force to be reckoned with on the battlefield.

Leo could plainly feel the Dark Mage's power. It dwarfed his magical abilities. The mere fact that he could float across the ground, untethered to the earth spoke volumes of his magical strength.

The mage floated right up to the team, stopping around twenty yards away.

"Pathetic," he sneered at them. "You are all weak. I am going to enjoy destroying you. First, I shall cripple you all, then I will slowly dismember you, one by one. After that…"

Before he could continue, Leo pulled one of his throwing axes out of his Inventory and threw it as hard as he could at the mage,

The weapon spun through the air and struck the orc right in the center of his forehead with a sickening crunch.

His eyes rolled back in their sockets and he keeled over. Dead before he hit the ground.

"Fucking douchebag," grunted Leo. "Why do these super-evil fuckers always think they gotta revel in their own glory before they do anything. What an ass. Come on, let's see if there's anything worth looting here. I doubt it, it you never know."

Jane burst out laughing. "Well, that was a bit of an anticlimax," she said.

Everyone joined in with her mirth. Partly out of amusement, and partly out of sheer relief that the quest was now truly over.

CHAPTER 27

Leo stood alone, balancing easily on a broad branch of one of the gigantic trees in the Sacred Grove. The trees were unlike any he had seen before, in that not only were they massive, but they were also hollow inside. The interior of the trees was like apartment blocks. Each one contained several large private dwellings.

Leo checked out his Stat sheet. The numerous Corrupted Orcs he had killed, plus his solo killing of the high-level Orc Dark Mage had shot him up by 3 Levels, and he now stood at Level 68.

He put his 15 points into Dexterity, because he didn't want any of his Stats falling too far behind the rest. They hadn't got any loot that was worth taking. The orcs' weapons were all crap and anything the Dark Mage had on him was so corrupted by evil that no one wanted to touch it.

But on the plus side, all of the team was now at Level 15, bar Buck who had jumped to Level 16.

The team stood in a spacious clearing below. They were all in high spirits, having just defeated the Darkness that had been lurking in the woods. Joining them in their celebration were several ents, sprites, and dryads, all of whom were equally thrilled with the victory. The atmosphere was lively and festive, with plenty of libations being poured and an abundance of delicious vegetarian food and fruits available for everyone to enjoy.

But Leo felt like being on his own to think.

When they had arrived back at the glade to inform Everbark about the success of their quest, Willow had taken him aside and begged him to take her on as another disciple.

At first, Leo refused, even after she had pointed out what a good scout she would make, plus her various nature and earth spells could help with their very survival.

But then he had glanced at his screen, and he saw that although the notification regarding his quest to end the Darkness had gone, the disciple quest now said - **Train your *five* disciples to become better warriors.**

So, he had no choice but to accept.

But for the first time, he stopped taking the occurrence as a mildly amusing anomaly, and he realized that he was truly becoming some sort of cult leader. And that fact disturbed him. Greatly.

Leo's mind wrestled with conflicting emotions. Willow's plea to become his disciple echoed in his thoughts, stirring a sense of obligation within him. He had initially resisted because he was hesitant to take on the mantle of leadership that seemed to be thrust upon him. Yet, the words of the quest notification lingered in his mind, a stark reminder of his newfound responsibilities.

With a heavy heart, Leo acknowledged the reality of his situation. He had unwittingly become a figure of influence, drawing others to him with his high Charisma Stat. The thought unsettled him, stirring a sense of unease deep within his core. He had always preferred solitude, the quiet company of the forest over the clamor of followers.

But now, as the weight of his role settled upon his shoulders, Leo couldn't help but question his own desires and motivations. Was he truly meant to lead others, or was he simply a pawn in a greater game? The uncertainty gnawed at him, casting a shadow over the once-clear path ahead.

With a sigh, Leo clambered down the tree, finally ready to join the celebration.

As Leo descended from the tree, his footsteps muffled by the soft forest floor, he couldn't shake the nagging sense of doubt that lingered within him. Willow's hopeful expression flashed in his mind, her earnest plea tugging at his heartstrings despite his reservations.

"Hey there, fearless leader," Buck's boisterous voice broke through Leo's reverie as the burly warrior clapped a hand on his shoulder. "What's with the long face? We just saved the day, didn't we?"

Leo forced a smile, though it felt strained on his lips. "Just thinking, Buck. You know how it is."

Buck grinned, his eyes sparkling with mischief. "Ah, thinking. Dangerous business, that. Better leave it to the scholars, eh?"

The playful banter brought a fleeting moment of levity to Leo's troubled thoughts, but it did little to dispel the lingering doubts that clouded his mind. As they approached the heart of the celebration, the sights and sounds of the revelry enveloped them—the flickering glow of lanterns, the lively chatter of the gathered creatures, and the tantalizing aroma of roasted nuts and berries.

Jane, ever perceptive, caught sight of Leo's furrowed brow and offered him a reassuring smile. "You did good back there, Leo. We couldn't have done it without you."

Leo nodded gratefully, though the weight of his newfound responsibilities still pressed heavily upon him. "Thanks, Jane. I appreciate it."

As they mingled with the gathered inhabitants of the Sacred Grove, Leo couldn't help but feel a sense of displacement amidst the celebration. Despite the camaraderie and warmth of their companions, a part of him longed for the quiet solitude of the forest, away from the burdens of leadership and the expectations of others.

Lost in his thoughts, Leo found himself drifting towards the outskirts of the gathering, seeking solace in the embrace of the towering trees that surrounded them. The soft rustle of leaves overhead and the gentle whisper of the breeze offered a momentary respite from the clamor below, though the nagging doubts that plagued him remained ever-present.

As the night wore on, Leo remained lost in his thoughts, grappling with the weight of his newfound role and the uncertain path that lay ahead. Despite the celebration that continued to rage around him, he couldn't shake the feeling of reluctance that gnawed at his soul, wondering if he was truly cut out to be a leader.

He felt the raw power of Everbark approaching, the massive ent surprisingly silent for such a large creature. But then he was a part of the forest, so Leo supposed it gave him an advantage when walking amongst the trees.

Everbark stood silently next to Leo for a couple of minutes, taking in the beauty of the surrounding forest.

Then he spoke.

"I never asked you," he said. "Who was the drus you became tree-bound to?"

"Mossweaver," replied Leo.

Everbark chuckled. "Ah, yes. I suspected I felt echoes of his aura in you, but I had to ask to make sure. How is that young scamp?"

Leo laughed. "Young, seriously? He used to call me child."

"He is barely six hundred years old," said Everbark. "We drus can live to be several thousand years of age. So, to me, Mossweaver is the child."

Leo listened to Everbark's words, finding a sense of comfort in the ancient ent's presence.

Despite their differences in age and experience, there was a kinship between them that Leo couldn't quite explain. As they stood together beneath the canopy of the sacred grove, surrounded by the gentle rustle of leaves and the distant murmur of celebration, Leo felt a sense of peace wash over him.

"Mossweaver is... well, he's Mossweaver," Leo replied with a wistful smile. "Always eager to push the boundaries of what's possible. He taught me everything I know about mana control. As well as fighting forms, and how to conduct yourself in battle. But he also taught me to have a deep reverence for the natural world."

Everbark let out a rumbling laugh, the sound echoing through the grove like the gentle rumble of distant thunder. "Aye, that sounds like Mossweaver, all right. Always testing the limits of his powers, yet never forgetting the importance of respecting the balance of nature. As far as ents go, he is an anomaly. On the whole, we do not approve of violence, on the other hand, I freely admit that we will let others do violence on our behalf. Much as you did.

"Mossweaver disapproved of that dichotomy. He maintained that we should fight our own battles. That is one of the reasons he requested a position in a tutorial dungeon. Firstly, to hone his own skills, and secondly, to improve his teaching skills."

Leo nodded in agreement, a pang of longing

tugging at his heart as he thought of his old mentor. Mossweaver had been more than just a teacher to him; he had been a guide, a friend, and a constant source of inspiration. Despite their occasional disagreements, Leo owed much of who he was to the wise old drus.

"He is a good man ... ent," replied Leo.

The ancient ent simply nodded in response, a knowing smile playing at the corners of his mouth. Together, they stood in silence, two beings connected by a shared reverence for the natural world and a deep respect for the bonds that bound them together.

CHAPTER 28

The team had stayed overnight with the ents, sprites and dryads, and had left at sunrise, heading south.

"We need to find more humans," said Leo. "It's ridiculous, there were loads of decent-sized towns round here. They can't all have just disappeared."

"Does your map help at all?" asked Jane.

Leo shook his head. "It updated to show us the Lost City dungeon, but since then it's back to just showing me where we've been."

"Well then, I suppose all we can do is get walking and see what happens," said Buck. "I mean, it's not like we got anything better to do."

Leo chuckled. "True."

As the sun rose above the horizon, the forest was bathed in a warm and gentle glow. The rays of sunshine filtered through the lush canopy of trees, casting a mesmerizing pattern of shimmering golden light on the forest floor. The surrounding wildlife awakened to the morning light, and the forest was alive with the sweet sound of birds chirping and the gentle rustling of leaves, creating a peaceful and harmonious atmosphere.

As they walked, Willow, now a disciple, flitted alongside Leo, her iridescent wings shimmering in the sunlight. "Do you think we'll find any humans soon?" she asked, her voice tinged with curiosity.

Leo shrugged, a hint of frustration evident in his voice. "I hope so, Willow. It's strange how deserted these lands seem to be. I mean there's not even a sign of any mobs."

Buck nodded in agreement, his gaze scanning the horizon for any sign of civilization. "You'd think we'd at least stumble upon a village by now," he remarked, his tone tinged with disbelief.

Jane sighed softly, her expression thoughtful. "Maybe there's a reason for all this," she mused, her eyes flitting to the map in Leo's hands. "Perhaps there's something we're missing."

Leo shook his head. "No, I don't think there's any strange reason or great mystery. I reckon it's just the usual System fuckery. Ninety percent or more of the population died, so I suppose there's just a lot less of everything. Although I would have expected some more signs of life, like elves or dwarves or something."

The team continued walking, stopping for a lunch of fruit and nuts, and then continuing on until nightfall when they set up camp.

Leo spent the last hours of sunlight taking the team through his usual practice of meditation and mana control, then they cooked a brace of large squirrel-type creatures Leo had shot earlier that day and kept in his Inventory.

Willow had been less than happy with Leo's killing of the forest creatures, but she accepted that the rest of the team couldn't survive on just fruit and nuts, they needed protein. And with their System-enhanced bodies, they needed a lot more calories than they had before.

The next morning, they set off bright and early once more.

"You know something," said Leo. "I never thought I'd say this, but I'm getting a bit sick of this forest. And the snow. I know it's real beautiful, but come on, enough already."

"I've never been out of the forest," said Willow.

"Wow," said Leo. "But then again, this isn't the same forest you grew up in. I mean this isn't your world, it's some System hodge-podge of a load of different worlds. I think."

"That may be true," conceded Willow. "But the sacred grove is the same. And there are enough similarities to make it feel like home. I just can't imagine a place without trees. Although I would like to experience that, however strange the concept is."

As Leo and his team continued their journey through the dense forest, they couldn't help but notice the gradual transformation in their surroundings. The towering trees that had once loomed overhead and provided them with abundant shade and cover, began to dwindle in size as they moved further. Their branches became increasingly sparse, and their trunks started to slenderize.

With each step they took, the environment around them changed, and they found themselves surrounded by trees of modest stature. They were much shorter, and the canopy was less dense, letting in more sunlight. The team halted for the night and set up camp in the midst of these trees that now cast long shadows, adding a sense of eerie calmness to the already fading light. And it was obvious that they were now on the very edge of the forest.

As the night gave way to dawn, the sun slowly rose in the sky, casting a warm golden glow over the landscape. The group emerged from their makeshift shelter, and as they stepped out into the open plain, they were greeted with a breathtaking view.

The vast grasslands stretched out before them, dotted with clusters of trees and shrubs. The air was crisp and fresh, carrying the scent of the earth and the distant mountains. In the distance, the imposing silhouette of the mountain ranges rose against the horizon, their jagged peaks reaching up to the sky, crowned with a dusting of snow. The panoramic view was truly awe-inspiring, and the group couldn't help but feel a sense of wonder and excitement as they gazed out at the stunning landscape before them.

Willow's eyes widened in awe as she took in the sight before her. "It's... breathtaking," she whispered, her voice filled with wonder. "And a

CRAIG ZERF

little scary. So much open space."

"No worries," said Bradley. "It's just like the forest, except no trees."

"Which means it's nothing like the forest," said Jane, rolling her eyes.

The breakfasted on fruit once again, and then set off. Willow flew close to Leo, trying her best to hide her nerves.

Sometime just before midday, Leo held up his hand. "Stop," he said. "My mana awareness has picked up a number of somethings about a mile out. Flying low to the ground. Whatever they are, I'm not getting a good vibe. I reckon we got trouble approaching, so ready yourselves."

"There," Willow pointed, her eyesight superior to the rest of the team's.

"What the hell?" said Leo as he used Identify.

Plains Harpy – (Level 62)

Strengths -

Agility: Harpies possess exceptional agility, allowing them to maneuver swiftly in the air and evade attacks with grace.

Flight: With their powerful wings, harpies can take to the skies, giving them an advantage in aerial combat and allowing them to attack from above.

Sharp Talons: Harpies have razor-sharp talons on their feet, which they use to slash and tear at their prey with deadly precision.

Screech Attack: Harpies can emit a piercing screech that disorients and deafens their opponents, making it difficult for them to focus or retaliate.

Weaknesses -

Fragility: Despite their agility, harpies have relatively fragile bodies, making them vulnerable to sustained physical attacks.

Close Combat Vulnerability: While formidable in aerial combat, harpies are less effective in close-quarters combat, as their bird-like bodies are not well-suited for ground-based fighting.

Susceptibility to Elemental Attacks: Being part-bird, harpies are vulnerable to attacks that exploit their avian nature, such as electrical shocks or wind-based spells.

Limited Intelligence: Harpies are often depicted as creatures driven by instinct rather than intellect, making them susceptible to traps and cunning tactics devised by their opponents.

Harpies are fearsome creatures, combining the features of a woman and a bird. Their upper bodies resemble that of a human female, while their lower bodies transform into powerful bird-like appendages, including wings and taloned feet. These creatures are agile and swift, capable of soaring through the skies with ease.

Overall, harpies are formidable opponents in

the air, utilizing their agility and sharp talons to dominate the skies. However, they have weaknesses that can be exploited by clever and resourceful adventurers.

The peacefulness of the surroundings was abruptly shattered by the high-pitched cries of the Harpies. Their sharp, piercing screams sliced through the air like razor blades, making it nearly impossible to concentrate on anything else. With every flap of their wings, the noise grew louder and more unbearable, creating a deafening symphony that echoed across the plain. The rush of air produced by their descent whipped through the tall grass, causing it to sway and tremble violently, creating waves that rolled across the landscape. As the Harpies closed in on the team, the rush of air became even more intense, obliterating all other sounds and enveloping the area with an ominous and foreboding aura.

Leo's heart pounded in his chest as he surveyed the battlefield, a sense of urgency coursing through him. He knew they had to act fast to fend off the Harpies and protect his companions. Beside him, Bradley clenched his fists, his jaw set in determination, ready to unleash his magic upon their foes.

Leo quickly assessed the situation, his eyes scanning the swirling mass of Harpies overhead. With a determined expression, he raised his hands, channeling his mana he unleashed his

Whirlwind spell, summoning a mighty gust of wind that roared to life around him.

The invisible force tore through the air, whipping up debris and sending it swirling into a vortex of chaos. As the winds grew stronger, the Harpies faltered in their flight, their wings struggling against the powerful currents, causing many of them to plummet to the ground.

Leo gritted his teeth, pouring every ounce of his concentration into maintaining the spell, his muscles straining with the effort as he fought to control the tempest he had unleashed.

With a serene determination, Willow directed her focus toward the earth beneath her feet. Drawing upon the ancient magic that flowed through the land, she began to weave intricate patterns in the soil, her hands moving with a graceful precision. As she uttered a whispered incantation, the ground trembled beneath her touch, responding to her command.

Suddenly, tendrils of verdant green burst forth from the earth, twisting and coiling like serpents as they reached out to ensnare the fallen Harpies. The vines slithered across the grassy plain with an almost sentient grace, wrapping around the creatures' limbs and wings with a vice-like grip. With each movement, the vines tightened their hold, constricting the Harpies' movements and rendering them helpless against their verdant prison.

With a fierce battle cry, Buck surged forward,

his spear gleaming in the sunlight as he charged into the fray. His movements were swift and decisive, his recent training with Leo evident in every fluid motion. With a powerful thrust, he impaled the trapped Harpies with unerring accuracy, his spear cutting through the air with lethal precision. With each strike, he dispatched the creatures with a single blow, his strength and skill proving invaluable in the heat of battle.

Meanwhile, Bradley conjured torrents of fire with a flick of his wrist, the flames dancing and crackling with an infernal heat. The scent of singed feathers and burning flesh filled the air as the Harpies writhed in agony, their shrieks of pain drowned out by the roar of the flames. Bradley's face was a mask of concentration as he unleashed his fiery onslaught, his eyes alight with the thrill of battle.

Amidst the chaos, Lyra darted between the trapped Harpies with uncanny agility, her daggers flashing in the fading light. Her movements were a blur of speed and precision as she danced through the melee, her strikes finding their mark with deadly accuracy. With each well-aimed blow, she dispatched the creatures with ruthless efficiency.

But the battle was far from one-sided. The harpies were fast and remarkably agile. And Leo's whirlwind spell was still at a relatively low level. So quite a few of the flying creatures managed to get through his defenses and use their razor-sharp talons to inflict serious injuries. Deep cuts to his head and shoulders.

But Jane stood steadfast on the outskirts, her hands glowing with the gentle light of healing magic. With each wave of her hand, she sent soothing energy rippling through the air, bathing her companions in its warm embrace. The scent of earth and herbs mingled with the acrid tang of smoke as she worked, her focus unwavering despite the chaos around her.

With the final echo of battle fading into the distance, the plain fell into a serene stillness, broken only by the gentle rustle of grass in the breeze. Leo and his companions stood amidst the aftermath of their victory, their chests rising and falling with the rhythm of exertion. Despite the fatigue that weighed heavy upon them, there was a sense of triumph in their hearts, a testament to their unwavering resolve and steadfast unity.

As they surveyed the scene before them, a sense of accomplishment washed over them, filling them with a quiet sense of pride. The fallen Harpies lay scattered across the grassy expanse, their once-menacing forms now still and lifeless in the fading light. Around them, the landscape stretched out in all directions, a vast expanse of untamed wilderness waiting to be explored.

"Well, that was fun," Buck remarked, wiping sweat from his brow with the back of his hand. "Nothing like a bit of aerial combat to get the blood pumping."

"Speak for yourself," Lyra retorted, a playful

grin tugging at the corners of her lips. "I don't know about you, but I prefer my battles to be a little less... airborne."

Leo chuckled, a weary but satisfied smile spreading across his face. "Well, whether you like it or not, we certainly made short work of those Harpies. Another victory for the books."

"Indeed," Bradley agreed. "Now it's time for some looting."

The team got a selection of loot from the defeated harpies. Willow explained the uses and value of the various items.

Harpies' Feathers she said were prized for their magical properties and could be used in potion-making or as components for crafting enchanted items.

Harpies' Talons were sharp and durable and could be fashioned into potent weapons or sold to merchants for a handsome sum.

There was also quite a hoard of gold coins and precious gemstones, and there was no need for Willow to explain those.

But most important was the XP and the points gained. After all, Levelling up was paramount, and combat was the only real way to do that.

Bradley was now a Level 17 Flame sovereign.

Jane, a Level 16 Life warden.

Buck had jumped up to being a Level 18 Vanguard.

And Lyra, a Level 17 Shadowblade.

Leo had gained one Level, and he was now on

Level 69. His Whirlwind spell had also gained a couple of Levels and was now a Level 3 spell.

He put the 5 points into Intelligence and then led the group from the area. Keen to get away from the piles of dead bodies.

CHAPTER 29

The Great Falls Police Department has just over one hundred employees.

The RPG apocalypse hit Great Falls hard, killing over ninety percent of the population, but due to some random quirk of fate, eighty-two police personnel survived. Many with their families.

The ranking officer left alive was Police Commander Derek Garbo, Garbo quickly took charge of the station. There were only thirty-six police officers in the station at the time. He gathered them together, opened the armory to discover that their former stock of 9mm pistols, a mix of Bushmaster AR15's and Benelli shotguns, and full tactical gear including webbing and body armor, had been turned by the System into something else.

They now had racks of crossbows, swords, daggers, spears, and a range of light and medium armor. There were even two Scorpions, massive oversized siege crossbows.

The motor pool had become a set of stables, complete with a dozen horses and riding tack.

The sudden turn of events left everyone present in a state of confusion, and it took them more than a few minutes to process what had just happened. The atmosphere was tense, and people were struggling to come to terms with the gravity of the situation. However, the Commander, being a strong and capable leader, managed to maintain a level head and keep everyone together. Some were seen wandering around in a dazed state, while others were visibly shaken by the turn of events. Despite this, the majority of those present pulled themselves together and worked towards a common goal, displaying a remarkable level of cooperation and teamwork.

After carefully reviewing the list of personnel who were able to ride, the commander conducted a thorough assessment of the individuals who had family members residing in close proximity to the station. Based on this information, he put together two teams of highly skilled and competent personnel to venture out and check on the welfare of these families, with the primary goal of rescuing any survivors who might be in need of assistance. The commander specifically instructed these teams to keep an eye out for any form of transportation that could be horse-driven, such as wagons or carts, as this could potentially help speed up the rescue process and ensure that the survivors were safely transported back to the station as quickly as possible.

The Commander gave specific instructions to a

handful of foot patrols to scour the area and locate any remaining members of the staff who were still alive. The patrols were determined to carry out their mission and so they spent time familiarizing themselves with the weapons they had been provided, which were old but still serviceable. They made sure to wear the appropriate armor to protect themselves during their search. Once they were fully prepared, they set out on their mission, with a sense of purpose and determination.

Amidst the shifting landscape of their world, Commander Garbo made a strategic decision to relocate the headquarters to the Best Western Hotel. Positioned beside the river, it offered a vital resource in the form of fresh water, which had become essential for survival in the wake of the apocalypse.

Recognizing the importance of securing their new base, Garbo oversaw the fortification of the hotel. Metal shutters were installed to reinforce the windows, providing protection against potential threats. Barricades were erected around the perimeter, serving as a deterrent to unwanted intruders. Additionally, ample supplies of spike strips were laid out as a defensive measure against any approaching dangers.

With these measures in place, the Best Western Hotel transformed into a stronghold, offering safety and security to the survivors who sought refuge within its walls. It stood as a beacon of hope in a world plunged into chaos, providing a sanctuary amidst the uncertainty that surrounded them.

During this time, Garbo had taken in all eighty-two surviving officers, plus their extended families. Eventually, the hotel housed over three hundred of them. There should have been more, but the RPG Apocalypse had taken its deadly toll, leaving many without fathers, sons, sisters, or grandparents. Even with the reduced numbers, the former Best Western, which was now a four-story wooden inn with stables attached, fast became overcrowded.

As the number of survivors and their families swelled, the former Best Western hotel, now a four-story wooden inn with stables attached, quickly became overcrowded. The space that was once meant for a smaller number of guests was now bursting at the seams with people who had nowhere else to go. Despite the cramped conditions, Garbo made sure that everyone had a roof over their heads, food to eat, and a sense of security.

Then Garbo sent his officers out to find anyone else who needed sanctuary.

The town that was once a modern hub of activity, renowned for its C.M. Russell Museum and the scenic Giant Springs State Park, had undergone a dramatic transformation. What was once a bustling modern town was now a sprawling medieval city with an entirely different set of challenges.

The city was now devoid of basic amenities like running water, sewage systems, and electricity. The only two bridges that were once sturdy and reliable were now rickety wooden structures that looked like they could crumble at any moment, posing a significant risk to the safety of the people who used them.

After the initial chaos of the apocalypse, the officers found more survivors. As the trickle turned into a stream, the Commander realized that they needed more living space for the survivors, including police officers and their families, as well as civilians.

He decided to appropriate the nearby Hampton Inn, which was located next door. The inn was fortified by adding extra barriers and reinforced doors and windows. A chain link fence was also erected around the entire area to provide an extra layer of security and to keep any monsters out. The Commander made sure that the survivors had enough food, water, and medical supplies, as well as other necessities to sustain them in the short term. The Hampton Inn soon became a bustling hub of activity, with survivors coming and going, sharing stories, and working together to survive in this new reality.

After two months, Garbo was in charge of a small but thriving community of survivors totaling over five hundred people, and Garbo was at Level 10, where he had got his new class. He was now – surprise, surprise – a Commander. Before that he had merely ben a Warrior.

***

The Great Falls Criminal Institution (GFCI) was originally designed in the late 1940's as a low-security prison for minimum custody level inmates. However, since then the facility has been upgraded many times and is now called a Maximum Security establishment, housing over two thousand inmates in four separate blocks. These inmates range from relatively low-level inmates, all the way through to lifers who will never see the outside of the prison walls again.

Well, that was the plan. Until the RPG Apocalypse struck and all of the electronic locks in the prison failed at the same time. As well as the complete lack of security, the building went from a secure steel and concrete structure to a large medieval jail with dungeons.

It is a common misconception that the guards are in charge of what happens in a maximum-security prison. But in reality, there are certain inmates that have much more power than any of the aforementioned wardens.

One of these such inmates was a middle-aged man called, Scott Scott. A man so good they named him twice. Actually, Scott Scott was a complete psychopath. There are four possible subtypes of psychopathy – borderline, narcissistic, sadistic and antisocial.

Scott Scott was not borderline.

Serving six life sentences for the six murders that had been proven (there were another fourteen that had yet to be discovered), Scott Scott was an average-looking male, five feet eleven, well built, slightly receding hairline, close-cropped beard and mustache, and eyes of the very palest blue. Almost the color of glacial ice.

Scott Scott was also possessed of a voice that any charismatic preacher would have given his soul to possess. A rich baritone that projected an earnest, caring, almost loving timber that made one feel as if the recipient of said voice was the most important person in the universe.

In fact, it would be fair to say that Scott Scott was a man loved and feared in equal parts. Well, perhaps the 'feared' side did slightly outdo the 'loved' side. What with the psychopathic tendencies and the penchant for unspeakable acts of violence and torture and wanton evil?

And now, just over two months after the event, Scott Scott was the uncontested king of the survivors of the former Great Falls Criminal Institution, now known to all inhabitants as – Scotts Haven.

And Scott Scott had officially changed his given moniker to – Great Scott. A process that had involved absolutely no irony, nor sarcasm on the new leader's part.

His name was Scott – and he was great.

Even the System agreed. When he had gained Level 10, his class had changed from **Rogue** to

Great Tormentor. He was now at Level 18.

End of discussion.

Great Scott had appointed himself a triumvirate of advisors, whom he referred to as his, Troika. Two of them were fellow lifers. The third, an ex-mafia accountant.

Great Scott referred to them by Christian names only. The lifers were Jeff (three concurrent life sentences for killing his entire family by tying them up and burning them to death). And Stan, four life sentences for a spate of serial killings involving blonde females between the ages of twenty-three and twenty-five. Sta was very particular when it came to both age and hair color.

Parker, the accountant, was also serving a life sentence. Because although he was ostensibly a number cruncher, he also had a penchant for murder. He maintained it broke the drudgery of everyday bookkeeping. Kept him sharp.

"Talk to me, gentlemen," said Great Scott. "Parker, let us start with you. I would like a full review of our current weapons and general supply status."

"Not much of a change from last meeting," answered Parker. "Our gatherers have collected more canned foods. We have the smokers going and have managed to smoke and reserve a large amount of meat. Mainly dogs, and some cats. We have also tried to preserve some of the monsters that are roaming the area. Some are palatable, others not so much."

"Weapons?" asked Great Scott. "Again, no real change. Crossbows, spears, a ton of those spiked clubby things, some armor. Looks like the System replaced like with like. All the guards had batons, and those become the spiky clubby things Still, only enough to arm half the men."

"Has anyone come across any heavy weapons, catapults, that sort of thing?"

Parker shook his head.

Great Scott drummed his fingers on the table as he thought. "Unacceptable," he grunted. "We need more firepower. Have you sent people to check all of the military bases?"

"There are none left standing," said Parker. "And as you know, the police swept up all of their munitions very quickly after the strike. One must hand it to whoever is in charge, they're one smart cookie."

"I agree," conceded Great Scott. "However, we need more firepower if we are to expand our holdings. And the most obvious way to get more is to take it from the pigs. Jeff, what intel we got on the piglets?"

"Not much," admitted Jeff. "But it shouldn't be difficult to get some. All we need to do is send in a couple of our men to gain access to one of the cop's enclaves. They can gather some serious inside intel."

"How do we get them in?" asked Great Scott.

"Easy. The coppers are all magnanimous-like. We just get a couple of our most fucked up looking dudes. Skinny, maybe injured, and they can just walk up to any of the enclaves and ask for sanctuary. The pigs will take them in. After they've been there a couple of days and gotten some solid intel, they just walk out. Simple."

Great Scott grinned. I like it. Make it happen."

Jeff nodded and stood up, leaving the room to do his master's bidding.

CHAPTER 30

"People," said Leo. "Lots of people."

His mana awareness had picked up signs of life. But unlike usual, this was from miles away. Much further than his usual range. He could only assume that was because there were so many souls. Over a thousand, easily.

"Come on," said Leo with more than a hint of excitement in his voice. "Let's speed up. Fast jog."

Leo pushed his team hard. He could have run much faster but made sure he kept to a pace that they could keep up, although impatience gnawed at him. He was keen to see how a large population of humans were doing in this new RPG world.

A wave of sadness washed over him as they ran. He would never have considered a thousand people to be a large population before the apocalypse. Even the smallest towns had more people in them. But now it was more humans than he had seen in one place since he had fallen into the tutorial dungeon.

Within ten minutes they had run almost four miles and the town itself came into view in the distance, still a mile or so away. It was no more than a sprawling medieval village. Wood, mud, and thatched cottages. Cobbles streets. Rickety wooden bridges across the river. There were no walls and no visible signs of people.

Oddly, there was a sign. It looked really old, rusted, and faded, the metal pole it was on, almost rusted through.

It read - **Great Falls. Pop 60000**.

Leo came to a halt. "Hold on," he said. "That can't be right. If memory serves, Great Falls was in the opposite direction to what we've been traveling."

"And why's the sign look so old?" questioned Bradley. "It's only been a few months."

Leo shrugged. "More System fuckery. Ours not to question why, I suppose. Let's press on and see what happening in the town."

They continued jogging towards the village when Leo raised his hand. "People, just ahead, in that cluster of trees. Sorry, I should have picked them up earlier, but my mana awareness is being overloaded right now. Looks like they're hiding, which means either they're scared, or it's an ambush."

"I'll take a look," interjected Willow.

"What if they see you?" questioned Jane.

Willow scoffed. "If I don't want to be seen, they won't see me." And she flew off.

Shortly, Willow returned. "Ten humans," she said. "Very scruffy. Long hair, beards, they've got the same writing all over their arms and faces, and they smell awful."

"Writing," questioned Bradley.

"Must be tattoos," said Jane. "And if they're all similar, it likely means they're either gang members or ex-cons."

"What weapons?" asked Leo.

"Some crossbows, a couple of spears and they all have maces," answered Willow.

"Okay, we can safely assume it's an ambush," said Buck. "I say we go in all guns blazing. Metaphorically of course."

"Right, look we don't know how dangerous these guys might be," said Leo. "So, I'm gonna take point on this one. The rest of you, hang back. I'm serious, guys. Okay, you copy?"

The team nodded, although they didn't look happy about it, particularly Buck, who liked to be in the midst of any battle.

Leo equipped his axe, rolled his neck to loosen up his shoulders, and sprinted at the ambush.

The team, who had never actually seen their leader at full speed, were all open-mouthed in astonishment. He moved so fast that he was a mere blur against the landscape. He covered the three hundred yards in as many seconds.

The thugs didn't have time to launch their ambush before Leo was amongst them. And it was like a natural disaster. A tsunami of violence. If anyone tried to hide behind a tree, Leo's mana-enhanced axe simply clove through it, then a follow-up swing would either dismember or decapitate the bandit.

Two of them managed to fire their crossbows, but Leo smacked the bolts away with casual contempt, his movements so fast as you would miss it if you blinked.

It took the Level 69 Stormcaller Archmage-Hunter a mere seven seconds to dispatch nine of the bandits. He kept the tenth one alive for questioning.

Seeing the short, but vicious battle was over, the rest of the team approached. Their body language and general demeanor made it obvious they were shocked. They had known that their mentor was faster and stronger than they were, but before now they had never seen him use his prodigious skills. It was both humbling and scary as all hell. He was exponentially more powerful than them. Than all of them put together, actually.

He wasn't a human, he was a wrecking machine. A one-man weapon of mass destruction.

Leo walked towards them, dragging the single surviving bandit by his shirt collar.

"Well, they weren't exactly very skilled," said Leo as he threw the thug to the ground and placed his foot on his neck to keep him there. "None of them were above level 7. Should have left them up to you guys, but better safe than sorry."

No one spoke, all of them still struck dumb by the massive show of force they had just witnessed.

"Finally, Bradley said something. "Hey, boss," he began. "That was some serious shit. You took

CRAIG ZERF

out ten dudes in a couple of seconds."

"Nine actually," corrected Leo. "This idiot is still alive. Also, was closer to five or six seconds, not two." Leo looked down at the prone bandit. "So, asswipe, what you got to say for yourself?"

"Fuck you."

Leo shook his head. "Not very polite," he said, leaning down and snapping one of the man's fingers.

The man screamed in pain.

"Don't expect any mercy from me," said Leo. "You and your fellow assholes were going to kill us, so fuck you. Now, talk to me, where you from? Are you part of a larger setup? Why were you out here, I mean obviously you didn't know we were coming, so I assume this botched ambush was an attempted crime of opportunity."

"I won't tell you nothing. You have an idea of who you're fucking with. Great Scott is gonna tear you a new asshole, then he gonna give the girls to the men, and they gonna wish they were dead."

Leo sighed. "Now, you see, I was fine with the rambling, but then you brought the girls up. And that was just nasty." Leo formed a small mana bolt and launched it. A finger-sized bolt punched through the bandit's right hand, leaving a hole about an inch in diameter.

Once again, he screamed in pain.

Then Leo did the same to his left hand.

"Okay, I'll talk," squealed the man.

Leo shook his head. "No, you had your chance.

Time for talking is over."

"Please," begged the thug. "I'll tell you everything I know. Everything, just stop punching holes in me."

Leo made a pretense of thinking for a few seconds, then he nodded. "Okay, answer the questions I already asked."

"We're from Great Falls, well… what used to be Great Falls. As you can see, it's different now. I serve under Great Scott, he's a Level 18 Great Tormentor. We run out of Scott's Haven. Used to be the Great Falls prison. We were out here on patrol, looking for survivors. That's all I know. We weren't gonna harm you, seriously. Just ask you some questions, maybe make you pay a toll."

"Bullshit," yelled Jane. "You said your friends were going to rape Lyra and me."

The bandit hung his head, avoiding eye contact with Jane.

"Where is this Scott's Haven?" asked Leo. "What side of town?"

The thug pointed east.

"What about other survivors?"

"There's an enclave of ex-cops and their families on the opposite side of the city," answered the bandit. "But Scott's gonna …" he stopped talking.

"Scott is gonna, what?" asked Leo, his voice full of menace.

The man shook his head. "Nothing, I swear."

"Bradley."

"Yes, boss."

"Burn this fucker's face off."

"With pleasure, boss," replied Bradley as he conjured up a small fireball, holding it in his hand."

"No, wait," shouted the bandit. "He sent some spies into the police enclave a few days ago. They came back with a bunch of info, and the Great one is gonna attack them today."

"What time?"

"I dunno. Midday maybe."

"Anything else?"

"No, I promise."

"I believe you," said Leo. And without warning he launched a mana bolt at the man's head. It punched a hole straight through, killing him instantly.

"Come on," he commanded his team. "Let's get going, see if we can't help these cops. But first, quickly loot the bodies, the more weapons we have the better, we got no idea what we're running into."

After collecting their loot, they ran off, heading for the west side of the town.

CHAPTER 31

"Get more men to the entrance," shouted Commander Garbo. "And I need the Scorpions there as well. Come on, let's move it."

The psychos from the prison were on their way to attack the police community. It was meant to be a surprise attack, but the Commander had constant patrols out, looking specifically for this sort of thing.

So, they had advance warning, and he had about half an hour to prepare for them.

He started by dragging a couple of wagons in front of the gate to reinforce them. Then he had his people drag out desks, tables, sofas, and mattresses. Because although they had a secure perimeter, it was just chain-link fencing, no solid walls, And the furniture would provide some cover for the defenders inside the wire.

As the officers scrambled to fortify their defenses, the atmosphere crackled with tension. The clang of metal against metal and the shuffling of furniture filled the air, punctuated by terse commands from Commander Garbo.

"Move those desks over there, quickly!" Garbo barked, his voice cutting through the chaos like a whip. "And grab those mattresses, we need more cover by the gate!"

The sense of urgency was palpable as the officers worked with feverish determination. Sweat beaded on their brows as they lugged heavy furniture into position, their muscles straining with effort.

Outside the wire, the distant sounds of approaching footsteps and loud whooping sent a chill down their spines.

Charlie Frost, Commander Garbo's 2IC stood next to him as they watched the horde of criminals come closer. "Must be over three hundred of them," he noted.

"Yep. Looks like they have a limited number of ranged weapons, from what I can see. Mainly maces, a load of spears, and maybe sixty crossbows."

"So, they going to want to get up close as fast as possible," said Charlie. "How many combatants do we have?"

One hundred and seven. The rest are children, or too old and frail. We are going to be stretched thin, but at least all of them have crossbows or longbows. Plus the Scorpions are going to have a big impact. I suppose a lot is going to depend on how many ranged spells they have."

"I've got water barrels dotted around the compound in case they lob fireballs at us and we need to put out some fires," said Charlie.

Garbo pointed. "Look, that's how they plan to breach the fence."

The horde had parted to reveal two large wagons with battering rams strapped to the front. Each was being pushed by ten men.

"Charlie, get the scorpions on to those ASAP," yelled the Commander. "If they pick up any speed and hit the gate, they will definitely break through. Also, anyone with any sort of ranged attack spells, tell them to join in."

Charlie sprinted off, shouting orders as he did.

The teams manning the two Scorpions at the gate turned them to face the incoming wagons, cranking back the arms and loading large iron bolts into the gutters.

With a thump, they both fired.

And missed.

Frantically the teams reloaded and adjusted their aim, this time both aiming for the same wagon as it picked up speed, getting closer by the second.

Again, the arms thumped up against their stops and the two iron blots flew forward.

One struck true, hammering into the front of the wagon, stopping its forward momentum momentarily, but not damaging it enough to put it out of action.

The second bolt missed again, but it did strike one of the criminals, punching through him to take out another three men before it stopped its trail of destruction.

By now the rest of the crowd of criminals were closer, just inside of crossbow range. Both they and the defenders opened up at the same time, and the air was filled with the fluting sound of crossbow bolts streaking toward their targets.

Then the first wagon hit the gates. They bent inwards but stayed solid.

As the second battering ram struck, the locking bar gave way with a resounding snap, and the gates were smashed open.

With relentless ferocity, the assailants surged forth, their features contorted in a primal display of fury as they bore down upon the defenders with unbridled aggression. Their footsteps thundered against the ground, stirring up clouds of dust that swirled in the air like a frenzied dance.

In stark contrast, the officers remained resolute, their faces set in grim determination as they braced themselves for the impending clash. Each one stood tall, their spears held aloft like a forest of steel, gleaming in the harsh light of day.

The tension hung thick in the air, palpable and electrifying, as the two opposing forces hurtled toward each other with unstoppable momentum. Time seemed to slow to a crawl as they closed the distance, the pounding of their hearts drowning out all other sounds.

With a deafening roar, the two sides collided in a cacophony of chaos, the clash of metal against metal reverberating through the air like thunder.

Spears met flesh with a sickening thud, sending sprays of blood arcing through the air in crimson arcs.

Sweat mingled with the scent of blood and fear, filling the air with a palpable tension as the defenders fought tooth and nail to repel the attackers. Each side pushed against the other with all their might, locked in a desperate struggle for survival.

Despite the overwhelming odds stacked against them, the defenders held their ground with unwavering resolve, their muscles straining with exertion as they fought all out to repel the onslaught. Each thrust and parry were executed with precision and skill, as they danced on the razor's edge between life and death.

Amidst the chaos of clashing weapons and shouted commands, Commander Garbo's voice pierced through the tumult like a beacon of authority. His words echoed across the battlefield, commanding attention and instilling a sense of unwavering resolve in the hearts of his men.

"Stand your ground!" he bellowed, his voice carrying the weight of authority and determination. "Hold the line!"

Each syllable resonated with power, cutting through the chaos and rallying the defenders to action. Garbo's words were a lifeline in the midst of the fray, a reminder of their duty and their purpose in the face of overwhelming odds.

As the battle raged on, his voice remained a

constant presence, guiding and inspiring his men to fight with valor and determination. With each shout, he fueled the flames of their courage, urging them to stand firm against the tide of enemies that threatened to overwhelm them.

The officers gritted their teeth, their hearts pounding with adrenaline as they fought with everything they had. Despite the chaos and danger all around them, a sense of determination burned bright in their eyes as they refused to yield to the assault.

However, soon the disparity in numbers began to tell, and the defenders were pushed back, allowing more and more of the criminals into the enclave.

"There's too many of them," Charlie yelled to the Commander. "We've lost seventeen people already and the perimeter's too large to hold. We need to pull back."

Even as he was speaking, Charlie didn't stop swinging his sword, slashing and hacking at the enemy.

"We can't pull back," answered the Commander. "The children are in the inn, if these bastards break through, they'll kill them all. Fucking reprobates."

But regardless of what needed to be done, the defenders simply did not have enough people to stop the seemingly never-ending horde of psychotic killers pushing their way into the compound.

It was only a matter of time, minutes maybe before the line gave way and the battle was lost.

"Charlie, choose ten men and send five to each inn as a last stand. Tell them to protect the children and the elders or die trying."

Charlie didn't react, instead, he started at the oncoming horde.

"Charlie, listen up," yelled the Commander.

Charlie raised his right hand and pointed. "What the fuck is that?"

The Commander turned to look and saw a small mound of earth being thrust up in the middle of the crowd of attackers. Like a miniature mountain. Then, without warning, the top blew off, and an explosion of red-hot lava spewed out, filling the air with loads of burning pieces of molten rock.

***

Leo called a halt and they stopped running. Perhaps a hundred yards in front of them was a horde of screaming, cussing, ululating men wielding maces, spears, and crossbows. And they were attacking a compound surrounded by chainlink fencing.

"I assume the bunch of howling lunatics are the bad guys in this scenario," he said. "Which would make the guys defending the compound the good dudes. So, let's go help the good dudes."

"There's a lot of bad guys," noted Bradley.

"Yep," agreed Leo. "What say I thin them out a

bit, I've been dying to try this new spell I got."

Leo called the spell up on his screen.

Pyroclasm (Level 1): subject can channel the power of a volcanic eruption, sending molten lava cascading down upon enemies, dealing massive damage over time.

He concentrated on it, and a circle with a cross in it appeared in his vision. Much like a telescopic sight. So he aimed at the center of the crowd of misfits.

Then, steadying himself, Leo unleashed the spell with a swift motion of his hand. A mound of earth pushed upwards in the middle of the horde. Then the air shimmered with heat as molten lava erupted from the ground below. Searing flames engulfed the enemy ranks, sending screams of agony echoing across the battlefield.

The smell of burning flesh filled the air, mingling with the acrid scent of smoke and sulfur. The ground trembled beneath their feet as the spell wrought devastation upon their foes, leaving a trail of destruction in its wake.

Bradley added to the destruction, casting a torrent of fire that washed across the enemy ranks, scorching and burning as it did.

As Leo's spell began to fade, he swiftly equipped his bow and arrow, his fingers deftly selecting an arrow from his quiver and he Imbued it with both Wind and Lightning. With practiced precision, he aimed at the heart of the attackers, his focus unwavering as he released the arrow.

It soared through the air, a streak of gleaming silver against the backdrop of chaos. As it found its mark, there was a deafening explosion of sound and light, sending shockwaves rippling through the enemy ranks.

Dozens of foes were caught in the blast, their bodies torn asunder by the force of the explosion. The air filled with the sharp tang of burnt ozone and the metallic scent of blood, mingling with the acrid smoke of battle.

Leo's arrows continued to rain down upon the enemy, each one finding its mark with deadly accuracy. With each explosion, more of the attackers fell, their numbers dwindling with each passing moment.

"Right," shouted Leo. "Time for a bit of meeting and greeting. Let's get up close and personal with these fuckers."

He equipped his axe, and Buck and he charged forth, slamming into the surviving criminals like a juggernaut.

The rest of the team held back, trusting in Leo and Buck's martial prowess.

CHAPTER 32

As the chaos unfolded before them, the defenders stood in awe of the devastation wrought by Leo's spell. The air crackled with the residual energy of the explosion, sending shivers down their spines as they watched the enemy ranks crumble before their eyes.

"I have no idea who those people are," yelled Commander Garbo, his voice barely audible over the din of battle. "But they just saved our asses."

Charlie's eyes widened in disbelief as he surveyed the scene before him. "Holy crap," he breathed, his voice barely a whisper. "That guy is an absolute monster. How the hell has anyone managed to get that freaking powerful?"

Garbo's jaw tightened with determination as he surveyed the chaos unfolding around them. "No idea, but let's give them a hand. Everyone, up and at them. Follow me."

With a resolute nod, Garbo charged forward, his spear held aloft as he carved a path through the now disorganized attackers. The rest of the defenders followed suit, their hearts pounding with adrenaline as they joined the fray.

With a collective roar, they surged forward, their weapons gleaming in the dim light as they clashed with the enemy. The clash of sword and steel reverberated through the air, mingling with the shouts and cries of combat.

Garbo fought with the ferocity of a lion, his spear a blur as he struck down any foe that dared to cross his path. Beside him, Charlie fought with equal determination, his movements fueled by a mixture of fear and adrenaline.

As the battle raged on, the defenders found themselves slowly gaining the upper hand. With each passing moment, they pushed the enemy back, driving them further and further away from the safety of their community.

As they got closer to the heart of the battle, they could now plainly see two men, one with a battle axe, the other with shield and spear. And they were like mobile slaughterhouses. The man with the axe in particular. His movements were so fast, and so coordinated it looked like trick photography.

Blood sprayed in arcs across the battlefield, and the sound of screaming agony and men pleading for their lives filled the air.

But the two men showed no quarter.

They continued their slaughter with an almost stoic implacability. There was no sign of enjoyment, they were simply doing a job of work.

Exterminating the wicked.

Finally, there was only a ring of five attackers

left. They stood with maces raised, and in the middle of the ring stood a single man. He was unarmed.

"Wait," he shouted, holding up his hand. "We need to talk."

Leo motioned for all to stop, and then he stepped forward. "Who the hell are you?" he asked.

The man looked genuinely puzzled. "You don't know?"

"Of course I don't know, you fucking donut," snapped Leo.

"I am Great Scott," the man said. "And I will make a …"

Great Scott never finished his sentence, on account of the fact that Leo had chopped his head off.

Buck finished off the five bodyguards, and that was that, the attack on the compound was over.

Commander Garbo approached Leo and held his hand out. "Greetings, stranger. I'd like to thank you and your companions for saving us all."

Leo smiled and took the Commander's hand. "Name's Leo," he said. "And we should be thanking you. That was an excellent workout, plus I reckon I probably got a ton of Levels out of it. Do you have any injured?"

"Many," admitted Garbo. "But we have a couple of healers, they're already hard at work."

"What Level?" asked Leo.

"3 and 4," replied Garbo. "They're quite high Level, because they've had a lot of practice. But even with them, we're going to lose a few people."

"Jane here is a Level 16 Life Warden," said Leo. "So, I don't reckon you're gonna lose anyone. At least not today."

"I'll get straight on to it," said Jane as she rushed off, seeking the wounded.

Both Garbo and Charlie stared at Leo.

"Level 16," gasped Charlie. "Are you shitting me?"

Bradley stepped forward, a cheeky grin on his face. He held out his hand and shook with Garbo and then Charlie. "Bradley," he said by way of introduction. "Level 17 Flame sovereign."

Buck smiled and followed suit. "Buck, Level 18 Vanguard."

Lyra rolled her eyes. "You boys are so juvenile."

Both Buck and Bradley laughed.

"And you are?" Garbo asked Lyra.

Lyra took his hand. "Lyra, Level 17 Shadowblade."

"And I'm Willow," said the sprite. "And I don't know any of you well enough to discuss my Levels."

Garbo and Charlie stared at the small magical creature, ther eues filled with awe and amazment.

"What Level are you then?" asked Garbo, urning back to Leo.

Leo chuckled. "Not important. What is important is looting these fuckers and then getting rid of the bodies before they start to stink up the place."

The Commander nodded in agreement. "Charlie, could you get a team onto that?"

"Right away, Commander."

Garo turned back to Leo. "Can I invite you and your team to the inn? We can talk, get something to eat and drink."

"I could eat," said Leo with a grin. "I don't suppose you got any beer?"

Garbo laughed. "As a matter of fact, we do."

Leo punched the air. "Hallelujah."

CHAPTER 33

Leo woke with a start. The night before, he and his team had eaten well and drank too well. In fact, he had partied so hard that he hadn't even checked his Stat sheet yet.

But a strident internal alarm had shocked him from his sleep as a raft of messages scrolled across his screen.

ATTENTION ... ATTENTION ... ATTENTION ...

You have reached Level 75 as such, you have been awarded a new class.

You are now a Magestorm Sentinel.

10 levels have been added to all Skills.

You have 100 extra points to allocate.

You have gained another Title – Protector of the People

As you are the first human to reach this Level, you have been awarded the rank of – Lord (20 points added to Charisma)

You have access to 2 new spells from your

spell book.

Thunderbolt Barrage: Summons a barrage of lightning bolts to strike down enemies from above, dealing heavy damage.

Shadowstep: Allows user to teleport short distances, granting them swift mobility in combat.

"Holy crap," gasped Leo. "I think that's all good news. Not sure about the whole Lord thing. Still, can't do me any harm I suppose."

He allocated 20 points to each Stat, bar Charisma, as he felt that was already high enough, and quite frankly he couldn't see any advantage to upping it even more.

Then he scrolled through the rest of the sheet.

Character Name: Lord Leo Armstrong (Human)

Class: Magestorm Sentinel

Titles: *Friend of the Elves*
Warrior Lord
Cyclops Slayer
Protector of the People

Level: 75

Experience Points (XP): 55300000/55000000

Stats:
- **Strength (STR):** 579
- **Dexterity (DEX):** 539
- **Constitution (CON):** 874
- **Intelligence (INT):** 539
- **Wisdom (WIS):** 614
- **Charisma (CHA):** 473

Stat points available - 0

Note - 5 Stat points are made available during each Level gained.

Skills:

- **Axe Throwing (Level 25):** subject is skilled in throwing axes accurately, dealing damage from a distance.
- **Survival (Level 25):** subject can navigate through wilderness, track animals, and find resources efficiently.
- **Archery (Level 38):** subject is proficient with a bow, allowing him to shoot arrows with power and accuracy.
- **Camping (Level 16):** subject excels at setting up camps, building fires, and surviving in outdoor environments.
- **Cooking (Level 17):** The subject can prepare simple and nutritious meals using

outdoor ingredients.

- **Axe Wielding (Level 45):** subject can wield an axe with a good degree of proficiency.
- **Lighting Infusion (Level 30):** subject can infuse his arrows with the power of a Thunderbolt.

Wind Infusion (Level 32): subject can infuse his arrows with the power of the Wind, this allows the arrow to travel further, faster and with more accuracy.

Spear Wielding (Level 30): subject is now proficient in spear combat.

Mana Manipulation & Core Control (Level 47): subject can now actively affect external mana.

Dagger Wielding (Level 14): subject can now use his dagger to deal death.

Whirlwind Spell (Level 13): subject can unleash a small whirlwind.

Pyroclasm (Level 11): subject can channel the power of a volcanic eruption, sending molten lava cascading down upon enemies, dealing massive damage over time.

Heal Over Time (Level 11): a weak healing spell that allows the subject to do a moderate amount of healing.

Thunderbolt Barrage (Level 1): Summons a barrage of lightning bolts to strike down enemies from above, dealing heavy damage.

Shadowstep (Level 1): Allows user to

teleport short distances, granting them swift mobility in combat.

Inventory:

- **Weapons:**
  - Throwing Axes (x2)
  - Battle Axe
  - Bowie Knife
  - Bow of Storms (Soulbound)
  - Quiver of Antiquity (Soulbound)
  - Starforged Spear (Soulbound)

- **Armor:**
  - Leather tunic with metal scales (Self-repairing, self-cleaning)
  - Vambrace (x2) (Self-repairing, self-cleaning)
  - Reinforced Leather Boots (Self-repairing, self-cleaning) Have been upgraded to provide extra Stealth
  - Stout leather trousers with metal scales (Self-repairing, self-cleaning)

- **Consumables:**
  - Healing Potion (2)
  - Rations (3 days)

- **Tools:**

- Flint and Steel
- Compass
- Climbing Gear

Miscellaneous:
- Map of the RPG Earth
- 760 gold coins
- 2 x Emeralds (Small)
- Verdant Moonlight Amulet (Rare)
- 5 x Iron Wolf pelts
- 1 x Drake meat
- 1 x Warg haunches
- 5 x Cured drake hide
- 2 x Drake claws
- 1 x Spell book

Quest Log:

Main Quest - The RPG Awakening:
- Investigate the transformed world.
- Level up.
- Do not die.
- Train your six disciples to become better warriors.

"Son of a bitch," he cussed. "Six disciples? Now who the fuck could that be?"

Shaking his head, he clambered out of bed, dressed, and went to wake the rest of the team.

CHAPTER 34

"My lord, as you know, my name is Charlie Frost, and I would like to become your next disciple."

Leo held his head in his hands. "Look, Charlie, I'd say no, but it looks like the System has already decided. Also, why did you just call me, lord?"

"There was a System-wide notification, my lord, informing everyone that you are the first human lord. Also, the highest-Level human in the world."

"Fuck," breathed Leo. "Way to attract unwanted attention. So, what does the Commander have to say about this?"

"He got a notification telling him to let me follow you, my lord."

"Okay, let's stop with the whole lord thing. It makes me real uncomfortable."

"Of course, my lord, right away."

Bradley chuckled. "I would just go with, Boss if I were you," he advised Charlie. "After all, one wouldn't want to irritate the most powerful man in the world."

The rest of the team laughed out loud, except

for Charlie. Instead, he looked vaguely affronted that they were taking his new master so lightly.

"Hey, Charlie," said Leo. "Don't sweat it. I'm just a guy."

Charlie shook his head, his expression deadly serious. "No. my lord," he said quietly. "You are not. You are so much more. You are hope. You are guidance. You are vengeance. You are our future."

And Leo stopped chuckling because he knew that was probably true.

Charlie took the knee, his head bowed in respect.

Buck followed, then the rest of the team.

A message flashed up on Leo's screen

Quest log update: Find more surviving humans and bring them back to Great Falls to start a thriving human enclave.

No time limit. But don't think you can just sit on your ass or there will be consequences.

Rewards: Once you have over one thousand inhabitants, the town will receive access to a System run shop.

"Okay, guys," said Leo. "Just got a quest from the System." He forwarded the message to the rest of the team.

"Well, it's not like we weren't going to do that at any rate," noted Buck.

"True," agreed Leo. "But now we get rewarded for it. Come one everyone, pack up and let's get going. Places to go and people to save. We leave in half an hour."

"Hoorah," said Bradley.

"Bradley," said Leo. "Don't do that."

"Sorry my lord."

Leo grinned. "Fucking asshole, now come one everyone, let's go do some good."

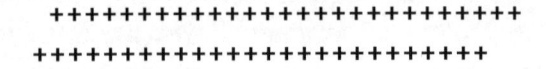

+++++++++++++++++++++++++++
+++++++++++++++++++++++++++

Thanks for sticking with me so far. Leo's adventure will continue in the next book – Level Up 3 Exploration.

A few quick points – firstly, if you follow this link, you can get a FREE novella.

https://dl.bookfunnel.com/tamg0r3pdg

Also – if you follow me on Facebook, you'll be kept up to date with new releases, news of more FREE book giveaways, plus loads of other interesting stuff.

https://www.facebook.com/craigzerfauthor

And – finally – if you're into LitRPG books – take a look at this one. It's a complete 3 book series. I've added the first couple of chapters here – then a link to the Amazon page.

And if anyone would like to chat, give me some feedback, or advice – please email me at…

craig@craigzerf.com

I will always get straight back to you.

Thanks again for all…

Your Friend in words

Craig

EARTH'S RPG OVERLORDS
Book 1 - COUNTDOWN
An Earth Apocalypse System Integration LitRPG Adventure novel

CHAPTER 1

"Damn it, Bonny!" Cash grumbled as he struggled to maneuver his wheelchair through the narrow doorway of their small, one-room hunting cabin tucked away in the Appalachian foothills. "Didn't I teach you how to open doors already?"

A soft whine escaped the massive Tamaskan dog, and she nuzzled her snout against the door handle apologetically, before stepping back to allow Cash room to navigate. The former army ranger's muscular upper body strained with the effort, sweat glistening on his forehead.

"Fuckin' prosthetics," Cash muttered under his breath, glancing down at the two carbon fiber legs that extended from above his knees, their titanium joints gleaming coldly. His left arm, also a sleek prosthetic limb, was currently detached and lying on a nearby table - an annoying necessity whenever he had to work on the blasted thing.

"Alright, girl," he said to Bonny, forcing a lopsided smile with the only half of his face that could still manage it – the right side. The left was a spider web of scars, like a gruesome road map of pain, extending up to the black eye patch that covered the empty socket where his left eye used to be. "Let's get this new project started."

Cash heaved himself out of the wheelchair and onto a cushioned bench, gritting his teeth as he did so. He was no stranger to discomfort, but the constant phantom pains in his missing limbs were a relentless reminder of the price he'd paid for his service.

"Hand me that wrench, will ya, Bonny?" he asked, reaching out with his remaining flesh-and-blood arm. To his surprise, the dog dutifully picked up the tool in her mouth and brought it to him, wagging her tail proudly.

"Good girl! You're getting better at this every day." Despite the pain, Cash's voice held warmth and affection. Bonny was more than just a pet; she was his lifeline in this isolated existence, the one constant source of companionship and love.

"Alright, let's see if we can't make these damn legs work properly." He began adjusting the tension in the prosthetic knee joint, his fingers expertly weaving around the intricate machinery. As he worked, Bonny settled down at his feet, her head resting on her paws as she watched him intently.

"Y'know, girl," Cash mused aloud, "I used to be able to run for miles without breaking a sweat, back before... Well, you know." He gestured vaguely to his missing limbs. "Now, I'm lucky if I can get to the end of the driveway without wanting to pass out from pain."

He sighed, pausing in his tinkering to rest for a moment. The challenges he faced daily were immense, but his stubbornness and determination kept him going. With each day that passed, each small success and failure, Cash fought to reclaim control over his life – even if it was only in the form of a well-adjusted prosthetic limb.

"Ah, fuck it," he grumbled, picking up the wrench once more. "Let's get back to work."

Once Cash had finished adjusting his prosthetics, he rose to his feet with a grunt and a grimace. Bonny perked up, her tail wagging and ears twitching in anticipation.

"Alright, girl, time for breakfast," he said, limping towards the small kitchen area as Bonny eagerly trailed behind him. He prepared a simple meal of eggs and bacon before setting down a bowl of kibble for Bonny. "Here you go, bitch," he chuckled, scratching her behind the ear as she dug into her food.

"Bon appétit, you ravenous beast," Cash muttered to himself as he chewed on his bacon. He knew it wasn't gourmet cuisine, but it was enough to keep them both alive and kicking – or hopping, in his case.

After finishing their meal, Cash fired up his computer and logged into his favorite online RPG game. It was one of the few ways he could escape reality, immersing himself in a world where he could walk, run, and fight without pain. Bonny curled up at his side, sensing that it was time for her human's daily gaming ritual.

"Let's see," he mused aloud, scanning the chat room for his teammates. "Who do we have here to make nice with OneArmedBandit 99?" It didn't take Cash long to get most of his team together. It wasn't a planned excursion, but most of them knew, if they were ever looking for a dungeon dive, Cash was pretty much always available.

As Cash coordinated with his virtual comrades, ordering them around the battlefield with practiced ease, Bonny snoozed by his side, occasionally twitching in her sleep as if dreaming of chasing squirrels.

"What's the problem, Bandit?" asked DeathKnight. "You drop your keyboard, or you cramping up on the controls? Get your head in the game."

"Hey, DeathKnight," Cash answered, smirking at the screen. "Ever tried fighting with the world's worst lag? Now, that's a challenge." He ignored the pained twinge in his own missing limb, focusing on the thrill of battle.

"Shit," he muttered, as his character took a devastating blow from an enemy. "Fucking arm." He slammed his good hand down on the table in frustration, causing Bonny to stir and fix him with a concerned gaze.

"Sorry, girl," he sighed, scratching her head apologetically after he had shut down his computer. "Didn't mean to upset you."

Throughout the day, Cash balanced his time

between gaming and tending to his and Bonny's needs – taking breaks to feed her, and clean up around the cabin. No matter how much pain he was in or how exhausted he became, he refused to ask for help. The thought of someone else witnessing his struggle, pitying him, made bile rise in his throat.

"Fuck that," he whispered fiercely, gritting his teeth as he started to lay a fire in the open stone fireplace.

"Who needs help when you've got determination and good ol' fashioned stubbornness?" He chuckled darkly, collapsing onto the floor beside Bonny, who licked his face affectionately.

After a couple of minutes, he slowly got to his feet, stomped over to the door and glanced outside, frowning as he did so. "Look at these fucking clouds, Bonny," Cash grumbled as he squinted up through the rough-hewn window of his cabin. "Looks like a storm's coming." The sky was a deep shade of purple, heavy with the threat of rain. A chill breeze whispered through the trees, rustling the leaves and teasing at his unkempt hair.

"Better gather some firewood before it hits," he muttered, giving Bonny a pat on the head before grabbing a tote bag for the wood and slinging it over his shoulder as he headed out into the Appalachian foothills. He gripped his crutch with his one good hand, feeling the familiar ache that came from relying so heavily on it for support. But he'd be damned if he let anyone else carry the load for him.

"Come on, girl," he called to Bonny over his shoulder, and she bounded eagerly after him, her tongue lolling happily from her mouth. They moved carefully through the undergrowth, Cash's eyes scanning the ground for suitable branches while his ears perked up at the symphony of bird chatter overhead.

"Ah, there we go," he said eventually, spotting a fallen branch just the right size for breaking down into kindling. It took him a moment to adjust his grip on the crutch, but determination fueled him, and he managed to snap off several pieces without too much trouble.

"Good girl, you found one too!" he praised Bonny, who had dragged a smaller branch over to him, tail wagging. She seemed to understand the importance of their task, and Cash's heart swelled with pride and affection for his canine companion.

"Can't believe how reliable you are, girl," he said, ruffling her fur. "You're like the goddamn canine version of me. Fuck, where's the sun gone?" he laughed, looking around as the clouds gathered even more ominously above them. "We better get this shit inside before we're both soaked."

As they hurried back to the cabin, Cash felt the first fat drops of rain splatter against his face. He unlocked the door and pushed it open, revealing the cozy, cluttered interior that was their home.

Bonny bounded in ahead of him, shaking herself dry as he followed, doing his best to keep his balance on the slippery floor.

"Alright, girl," he said, breathing heavily from the effort of their firewood-gathering mission. "Let's get this shit stashed away and curl up together by the fire." He could think of no better way to spend a stormy evening than with his faithful friend by his side, sharing warmth and companionship despite the cold, unforgiving world outside their door.

"Cheers to us," he muttered as he lit the fire, raising a glass of bourbon to toast their resilience. The flames licked at the logs, casting flickering shadows across the room and bathing them both in a warm, golden glow.

The fire crackled and popped, casting dancing shadows on the cabin walls. Cash stared into the flames, his thoughts drifting back to a time before the explosion that had changed everything. Bonny lay by his side, her soft, rhythmic breaths calming him as he let the memories wash over him.

"Hey, Stone! You gonna play poker with us or not?" Sergeant Carson's voice echoed in his head, a wry grin plastered on his face as they sat around a makeshift table in their tent in Afghanistan.

"Fuck yeah, I'm in," Cash replied, tossing a handful of chips into the pot. "Prepare to lose your ass, Carson."

Laughter erupted from the group, the

camaraderie between them strong and unwavering. They were a family, bound together by shared experiences, triumphs, and losses. Cash remembered the easy banter, the sense of belonging, and the knowledge that they would always have each other's backs. The thought brought a bittersweet smile to his face.

"Stone, you've got a horseshoe up your ass today," Corporal McHugh had said, slamming his cards down in defeat. "That's three hands in a row!"

"Maybe I should quit while I'm ahead," Cash had joked, raking in the chips. "Nah, who am I kidding? I'm going for broke!"

"Speaking of broke," Carson chimed in, "anyone else get a care package from home recently? My mom sent me some of her homemade fudge, and I'm willing to share... for a price."

"Your mom's fudge, huh?" Cash teased. "You know I can't resist it, but what's the catch?"

"Simple," Carson replied with a smirk. "Next time we're on leave, you take my sister out on a date."

"Deal," Cash had agreed without hesitation, shaking Carson's hand.

The warmth of the memory slowly faded, leaving him with an empty ache. The laughter, the companionship, the family he'd once known... all gone in an instant. The explosion had torn through his body and his life, leaving him broken and alone, a shadow of his former self.

"Bonny," he whispered, stroking her head

gently. "You're the only family I have left, girl."

As the fire continued to burn, he thought about the stark contrast between then and now. Once, he'd been part of something bigger than himself. Now, he fought daily battles just to make it through each day, his prosthetics a constant reminder of what he'd lost. The people who'd once filled his life were gone, replaced by the solitude of his Appalachian foothills cabin.

"Fuck 'em all," he murmured bitterly, feeling the weight of his isolation pressing down on him. "We don't need 'em, do we, Bonny?"

But even as he spoke the words, Cash couldn't shake the longing for what he'd lost. He missed the laughter, the friendship, and the sense of purpose that had defined his life before the explosion. And though he'd built a new life for himself, forging a bond with Bonny that ran deeper than he could've imagined, the ghosts of his past still haunted him.

"Cheers to us, Bonny," he said quietly, raising his glass once more. "Survivors against the world."

The sound of scuttling feet drew his attention and he glanced up to see a squirrel scamper across the floor. Theoretically, Bonny should be keeping the little fuckers away, but she knew that although Cash complained about the cute little furry rodents, he didn't actually mind them.

"Fuckin' squirrels," Cash chuckled under his breath, as he watched the little bastards scampering around his cabin. "I swear they're out to get me." With a grunt, he adjusted himself in the worn recliner, the prosthetic limbs shifting uncomfortably against his body.

"Bonny!" he called out gruffly. "Go chase those furry assholes away, will ya?"

With a bark of affirmation, Bonny tore off through the open door, scattering the squirrels in all directions. But as soon as they ran off, she stopped and came back inside, her face a huge doggy grin, tongue lolling out in pleasure and amusement.

Cash couldn't help but chuckle at the sight. It was a small victory, but it still brought a smile to his face.

"Who needs people when you've got a dog like you, huh, girl?" he mused, scratching Bonny behind the ears when she returned victorious. "You're worth a hundred fuckin' humans."

As the night settled in, Cash once again immersed himself in the online RPG world where he could forget, if only for a while, the reality of his situation.

"God damn, this game is addictive," he muttered, fingers flying across the keyboard as he navigated his virtual self through dungeons and battles. In this digital realm, he was whole again, a powerful warrior feared and respected by all who crossed his path. He reveled in the feeling of strength and control that had been ripped from him in the real world.

"Cash, my man! You ready for the big raid tonight?" a voice crackled over the headset, snapping him back to reality. It was Gary, one of his gaming buddies and the closest thing he had to a friend these days.

"Damn straight," he replied, trying to keep the bitterness from his voice. "Just let me grab another beer, and I'll be good to go."

"Beer and video games - the perfect combination," Gary chuckled. "Alright, man, see you in there."

As Cash logged off for a moment to fetch himself another cold one, he couldn't help but feel a pang of envy for those who could walk away from the game and return to normal lives, uninhibited by the scars of war. He knew Gary had no idea about the extent of his injuries, and he preferred it that way. It was easier to pretend everything was fine, even if just for a few hours each day.

"Bonny, sometimes I think this is it," he confessed to the dog as she lay by his side, always attentive and loyal. "This is all life's got left for me - a creaky old chair, some shitty online game, and a cabin in the middle of nowhere. Maybe I'm just biding my time until the end."

But as he looked down at Bonny, her trusting eyes staring up at him, he felt a surge of defiance building within him. It might not have been the life he'd envisioned, but it was still his life, dammit. And he'd be damned if he let anyone else dictate how he lived it.

"Fuck it," he said determinedly, cracking open

the beer and taking a swig. "I've survived worse than this, and I'll survive whatever comes next. Let them pity me, or ignore me, or whatever the hell they want. I'll live my life on my own terms, right here with you, girl."

And with that, Cash Stone, former army ranger and survivor against all odds, raised his glass in a silent toast to his steadfast companion and the defiant existence they shared, waiting for whatever lay ahead, together.

CHAPTER 2

The sun crept through the gaps in the curtains, casting a dim glow on Cash Stone's face. He groaned, feeling the weight of last night's bad drinking decisions pounding in his skull like an unhinged drummer. His eyes fluttered open to reveal a world that seemed far too bright for his liking.

"Fuck me sideways," he muttered, clawing himself out from under the sheets and then strapping his various prosthetics on.

He limped toward the kitchen, dragging his right prosthetic leg across the boards as his brain threatened to melt down and dribble out of his ears. Bonny watched him with concern, her ears flat against her head and her body tense. She let out a low growl, staring at something unseen.

"Alright, girl?" Cash asked, scratching her behind the ears. "You seem as fucked up as I feel."

With a grunt, he scooped porridge oats into a pan and set it on the stove. The air felt heavy, charged with static, making the hairs on the back of his neck bristle. Even the heat seemed oppressive, sticking to his skin like a second layer.

Altogether unpleasant.

"Christ, what is this weather?" he grumbled, stirring the porridge. "Last night, pissing with rain and cold, now it feels like I'm breathing soup."

Bonny whined, pacing around the kitchen, a ball of nervous energy. Cash frowned, keeping an eye on her as he poured his breakfast into a bowl. Something was definitely off, but maybe it was just his hangover playing tricks on him.

"Let's get some fresh air, yeah?" he suggested, hobbling out to the verandah with his bowl and a grimace. "Maybe it'll clear our heads."

The moment they stepped outside, Cash knew it wasn't just his hangover. The air was stifling, dense, like a thick fog had settled around them. He sighed, shoveling a spoonful of porridge into his mouth.

"Jesus, Bonny," he said between bites. "This weather's weirder than a six-legged cat. Feels like the air's gotten heavy or some shit." He chuckled, rubbing his temples. "Or maybe it's just my fucking hangover. Who knows?"

Bonny growled again, her hackles raised and her eyes darting back and forth. Cash frowned, setting down his bowl to crouch beside her.

"Hey, hey," he murmured, stroking her fur. "It's okay, girl. We'll figure this out, alright? Can't be worse than that time we found ourselves in a Tijuana bar with two hookers and a donkey."

Despite his attempt at humor, unease continued to claw at him as they sat on the verandah, the world around them strangely silent.

Cash couldn't shake the nagging feeling that something was off. He scanned the surrounding trees, searching for the familiar flash of bushy tails and chattering of squirrels. But there were none to be found.

"Bonny, do you notice something weird? The fucking squirrels are gone," he muttered, scratching his head. "Actually, it's quiet as a church out here. What the hell is going on?"

Bonny whined, her ears flat against her skull, her eyes wide with unease. It was as if the abundant wildlife that once surrounded their cabin had simply ceased to exist.

"Alright, this shit is just bizarre," Cash grumbled, finishing his porridge and standing up. "You know what? Fuck it. I'm gonna go--"

He never got to finish his sentence. Suddenly, a blinding white light enveloped them both, searing through his vision like a hot poker thrust into his eyes. Cash stumbled back, shielding his face with an arm as the world spun around him in a disorienting whirlwind.

"Jesus H. Christ on a cracker! What the fuck is happening?!" he yelled, his voice cracking with terror. Bonny barked frantically, circling around him as they both tried to make sense of the chaos.

The white light continued to burn, relentless in its intensity. Cash felt his heart hammering in his chest, thudding like a jackhammer against his ribs. Panic surged through him, and his thoughts raced, desperate for answers.

"Is this some kind of military experiment gone wrong?" he wondered aloud, his voice barely audible over the sound of his own pulse pounding in his ears. "Or maybe I've finally lost my goddamn mind."

As suddenly as it appeared, the light vanished, leaving Cash blinking away spots in the darkness, gasping for breath. Bonny continued to bark, her tail tucked between her legs, as they both struggled to regain their bearings.

"Bonny, you seein' this shit?" Cash rasped, massaging his temples as he tried to shake off the disorientation. He glanced around, waiting for something—anything—to make sense of the blinding light and the eerie silence.

Ahem. Attention, mere mortals of Earth.

A deep, resonant voice echoed in Cash's head, causing him to wince and grip his skull tighter.

We, the almighty Overlords, have a little announcement to make that will undoubtedly shake the very foundation of your puerile existence. Brace yourselves, for your world is about to undergo a transformation that will make your feeble minds spin.

First things first: in our infinite wisdom, we have decided to turn your dull planet into a colossal RPG game. Yes, you heard that right. Earth is about to become a sprawling playground of adventure, where quests and levels will replace your boring day jobs and mundane routines. Isn't that just dandy?

Now, here's a tidbit of news that might dampen your spirits. We regret to inform you that not everyone will make it through the initial adjustment period unscathed. Oh no, dear humans, some of you will meet your untimely demise within the next six months. And we are talking big time collateral damage. In fact, as many as ninety, to ninety-five percent of you buggers will shuffle in your mortal coils.

It's a bit of a necessary evil, you see—a culling of the weak, the clueless, and the boring. Think of it as a survival of the fittest scenario, but with a dash of RPG pizzazz.

But fret not, dear survivors! Once this integration period is over, Earth will undergo full Assimilation and become a "Free Zone" (cue dramatic music), open to all the races from the worlds under our control. Yes, you heard that correctly. Aliens, creatures, and beings from far-flung corners of the cosmos will grace your humble planet with their presence. Oh, the diversity! Oh, the potential chaos!

Now, here's the deal: any land and property not claimed by you humans within the allotted time will be up for grabs by the new immigrating races. And guess what? Not all of them are going to be warm and fuzzy. Some may resort to violence to snatch away land that they have no business claiming. It's like a twisted game of cosmic Monopoly, and you guys are in the hot seat.

So, here's a word of advice from your beloved Overlords: grow strong, humans. Flex those puny muscles and sharpen those wits. It's time to show those intergalactic interlopers that Earth is no pushover. The only way to protect what's rightfully yours is to toughen up, unite, and give those wannabe conquerors a good run for their money. Oh, and by the way, don't think that your vaunted technology is going to help you in any way at all, because ... the System has rendered it all null and void. That's correct, cars, weapons, electricity, computers, airplanes ... oh hell, you get the picture. Looks like we just got Medieval on your asses. (Pause for uproarious laughter).

In conclusion, dear humans, get ready for a wild ride. Prepare for quests, levels, and the imminent threat of extra-terrestrial squatters. Will you rise to the challenge and carve out your own destiny, or will you become cosmic roadkill? The choice, as always, is yours.

May luck favor the sassy and the strong. Happy adventuring!

The Overlords.

P.S. The system will initiate in 10 Earth minutes. So grab anything approaching a usable weapon and get ready for Armageddon.

"Fuck me sideways, I've gone insane," Cash mumbled, convinced that the hangover had finally pushed his brain past the point of no return. Bonny stopped barking, her ears pricked as if she was also listening to the strange voice.

"Wait a goddamn minute." Cash shook his head, trying to clear his thoughts. "Bonny, you can hear this as well? So, you're telling me that life is going to be like some fucking video game from now on?"

Nothing answered Cash's question. But there was no need, the announcement had been made and it was pretty self-explanatory.

"Shit, Bonny. We're screwed." Cash looked down at his dog, who gazed back with an expression that seemed to say, 'You're the one with the opposable thumbs, buddy.'

"Alright, System, or whatever the fuck you are," Cash said, straightening up and squaring his shoulders. "How about you tell me what my first move is? And it better not involve dancing on one leg while singing the national anthem."

Again - no response.

"Fan-fucking-tastic," Cash grumbled, rolling his eyes. He glanced up at the small gun cabinet next to the fireplace. Steel fronted and double locked, it contained two Colt 1911's and three hundred rounds of ammunitions. Cash hadn't bothered keeping a rifle as he was unable to use one with any accuracy due to his missing left arm.

"I reckon I'll check if those overlord fuckers are telling the truth," he said to himself. "Maybe they just bullshitting us all and firearms will work well enough."

He limped over to the cabinet, took the key from the chain on his neck, opened up and took one of the Colts out. It was already loaded. Cocked and locked and ready to rock and roll.

Cash pointed it out of the open front door and pulled the trigger.

Nothing.

He ejected a round and tried again.

Click.

"Shit, they weren't lying. What now?"

Cash gazed around the room. Finally, he saw his old ax. It was a two-handed lumberjack ax, and as a result, Cash had let it rust over. He could swing it using his right arm, but it was heavy and unwieldy. However, horses and beggars and all that shit. He grabbed the ax and rest it on his shoulder.

"Okay, Bonny," he stated as he checked his wristwatch. "Damned watch doesn't work. Obviously. I reckon that's about as weaponed up as we're gonna get. I guess we about five minutes away from the event horizon. Bring it on you fuckers."

He started counting down in his head, using the good old tried and tested one-Mississippi, two-Mississippi method. But before he managed to get six-Mississippi's out, the air reverberated to a loud roar and a brown bear came charging out of the forest.

The bear took one look at Cash and Bonny and attacked. As it bore down on them, Cash could see that this was no ordinary bear. It's eyes glowed bright red, like a pair of burning coals. Its teeth were so long they extended out of its maw like a saber-toothed tiger. And its claws looked more like steel knives than actual claws.

"What the fuck," yelled Cash. "I haven't finished my Mississippi's yet. It's not time, we still got at least a few minutes."

But it appeared the bear wasn't interested in Cash's problems as it lunged forward, its jaws snapping together like a steel trap, missing Cash's face by mere inches.

Cash responded by giving his ax an almighty swing. The weapon was difficult to control, but Cash gave it his all and he felt the blade sink deep into the bear's head. At the same time, Bonny sunk her teeth into the attacker's left leg, ripping at its tendons in an effort to cripple it and slow it down.

The bear howled in agony and struck out, it's one massive paw catching Cash just below his right arm. Cash was thrown across the verandah, hitting the wall of the cabin with such force the entire structure shivered like a bowl of Jell-O. He also felt at least three of his ribs shatter, and his back didn't feel so hot either.

With a grunt of effort, Cash staggered to his feet, faced the enraged bear, and swung for the fences. Once again, he hit a homerun and the head of the ax struck the bear right in the center of its forehead, sinking in with the sound of a hammer striking a ripe melon.

The bear's eyes crossed and it staggered backwards, only for Bonny to take the opportunity to rip another chunk of flesh from its right leg.

The bear stood still for a couple of seconds, swaying precariously, then it slowly started to sink to the floor, like a giant redwood being felled.

But before Cash could feel any sort of joy or thrill of achievement, the bear lurched forward, and with its final iota of strength, it slashed its razor-sharp claws across Cash's gut, eviscerating him with one vicious swipe.

Bonny took the opportunity to latch onto the bear's throat, and with a savage growl, she ripped it open, bring forth a geyser of blood.

With that, the bear fell to the floor, as dead as dead can be.

Cash likewise slumped to the floor, staring down as his entrails boiled out of his body. Bonny ran up to him, whining in concern and fear.

Cash smiled. "Sorry, Bonny," he said softly. "Looks like I'm well fucked. At least we showed that bear. You take care of yourself, you hear. Oh, and don't trust those overlord fuckers. Ten minutes until assimilation, my ass. They gypped us good and proper. No way that bear was any sort of normal animal."

Cash sighed and closed his eyes. Perhaps this

was for the best, he thought as he felt his consciousness slip away. After all, what chance did a cripple like him stand in this brave new world?

None, that's what.

And the world went dark.

https://www.amazon.com/Earths-RPG-Overlords-Apocalypse-Integration-ebook/dp/B0C9TYVWG5/ref=sr_1_10?crid=1RBC8T9I7AU4P&keywords=rpg+apocalypse&qid=1706094924&s=digital-text&sprefix=%2Cdigital-text%2C168&sr=1-10

Hit the link above to get the first book in the complete series.

Made in the USA
Monee, IL
31 July 2024